FORBIDDEN SNOW

RIVER R PALASEK

To my wonderful mother who was my support, proof reader, photographer, and first fan to this book. My journey here would have been nothing without you.
Love you always

Contents

PART ONE — 1

- **One** Barrel of Apples — 2
- **Two** The King's Attendant — 6
- **Three** Glittering Snowfall — 10
- **Four** Be Gentle With Beautiful Things — 13
- **Five** Secret Family Recipe — 19
- **Six** Cedric Draymoor — 23
- **Seven** Silk on Glass — 29
- **Eight** Protect the People Who Can Not Protect Themselves — 36
- **Nine** Why a Commoner, Corwin? — 40
- **Ten** You Will Find Your Peace Here — 46
- **Eleven** Dirty Dress — 51
- **Twelve** I Am Yours — 57
- **Thirteen** Thank You For Everything — 63
- **Fourteen** Forbidden Snow — 69

PART TWO — 73

- **Fifteen** Goodbye Brother — 74
- **Sixteen** The Garden — 79
- **Seventeen** Listen to Them — 82
- **Eighteen** Agnes — 86

Nineteen	What Kind of King Cries Like This?	94
Twenty	She Deserved Everything	98
Twenty One	Are You There?	102
Twenty Two	Mercy is not the Absence of Consequence	105
Twenty Three	Do I Have to be King?	115
Twenty Four	It is Gone	120
Twenty Five	Call me Corwin	125
Twenty Six	I am Not You	129
Twenty Seven	What Words Could Possibly be Enough?	133
Twenty Eight	Dear Reila	137
Twenty Nine	She is Still Here	140
Thirty	Thank You For Everything	145

PART ONE

One

Barrel of Apples

King Corwin Draymoor walked through the village, surrounded on all sides by armored guards whose silver-plated armor glinted beneath a pale, overcast sky. A cool breeze stirred the edges of his dark velvet cloak, deep red and trimmed with delicate embroidery, the hem just brushing the dirt path. He wore a gold crown with a single sunstone. Modest by royal standards, but unmistakably majestic. His expression was carved from marble: unreadable, distant, and faintly bored.

Children lined the narrow cobbled streets, some waving shyly, others simply staring wide-eyed at the man who had always existed only in stories. The scent of earthy smoke and baking bread drifted from the cottages, mingling with the faint tang of horse sweat and iron. Market stalls buzzed with life, potatoes in leaning pyramids, bolts of rough-dyed linen fluttering in the breeze. Their keepers bowed hastily as the royal procession passed.

The King barely glanced at the crowd. He had done this sort of tour dozens of times before. Smiling, nodding, pretending to listen to the cries of the people while his mind wandered to quieter rooms. It was all routine. Everyone he passed wore the same thin smile, the same lowered gaze, the same wave of fear. Their voices quieted at his passing, like wind swept through dry grass, hushed and uncertain. It exhausted him.

Then a cry of defiance rose above the others, cutting through the muttering like a blade. One of the villagers, a broad-shouldered man with soot-streaked skin and wild eyes, stepped forward, pushing past a kneeling neighbor.

"I bow to no man who hides behind steel and gold!" he exclaimed, "you sit in your stone palace while we starve and rot. Your crown means nothing to us." Whispers rippled through the crowd. Mothers pulled their children back, market traders ducked their heads pretending not to hear.

A few of the guards immediately stepped forward, hands on the hilts of their swords, chainmail hissing with the motion. One guard with a scar splitting his lip snapped, "on your knees, now, before you regret your tongue."

The villager did not move, "go ahead. Cut me down in front of your King. Show them all what his peace looks like."

The tension thickened. Even the horses grew restless, stamping the earth as if they sensed the threat. King Corwin did not flinch. His gaze did not even settle on the man. Instead, he looked away slowly and deliberately toward the rest of the villagers. He was only met with more bowing, more trembling, more fear.

Then he saw, kneeling beside a weathered **barrel of apples**, a girl sat with her head bowed low in respect. What caught his eye was not just her, it was the apples. Vibrant, red, and fresh. Too fresh for this region and too ripe for this time of year. The soil here was dry, the season wrong. It did not make sense. Curious, the King stepped forward. His guards tensed but held their ground when he raised a hand, signaling them to stay back. He walked up to the girl, stopping just in front of her. She remained still, kneeling, her hands folded neatly in her lap. He lifted her chin with the tip of his boot, forcing her to look up at him.

"Where did you get those?" he asked.

The girl looked up, her eyes wide but calm, "my aunt has an orchard about a hundred miles south of here, Your Majesty. I have just returned from visiting her and brought some back."

"A hundred miles south? That must mean she lives in the Montague Kingdom," Corwin had heard lots about the food that grows in the Montague Kingdom. They were known for their rich soil and flourishing harvest they had every year. He only had the honor to sample their feasts once when he was still prince. He had longed for a meal that good once more.

"Yes, Your Majesty," the girl replied with a gentle nod.

He looked back and forth between the apples and the girl curiously. She reached into her pocket and pulled out a handkerchief, carefully wrapping it around one of the apples. With both hands, she held it up to him without letting her skin touch the fruit. Not touching food meant for nobility was a simple courtesy, one often forgotten.

"Here," she said, "take one."

The King smiled as he accepted it, noting how unlike the others she was. While everyone else cowered or flinched at his presence, she remained composed and respectful, but unshaken. Obedient, but not afraid. His guards shifted behind him, armor clinking softly, unease rolling off them in waves. A king taking food from a commoner was unthinkable, dangerous, even. But they said nothing.

He lifted the apple to his lips and took a slow bite. The skin gave with a satisfying crunch, and sweet juice flooded his mouth. A crisp and cold sensation, with a hint of tartness near the core. It tasted of autumn, of orchard winds and sun-warmed fields, strikingly fresh compared to the waxy fruit served in the castle. He chewed slowly, savoring it, his eyes never leaving her face. Then, to the visible discomfort of his guards, the King knelt before her. His cloak pooled at his feet, as his crown caught the sunlight in fractured glints.

Before he could speak again, the girl quickly shook her head, "Your Majesty, you mustn't kneel in the dirt and soil your fine clothes."

Without hesitation, she pulled the shawl from her shoulders and laid it across the ground for him. The gesture surprised him. She was not doing it to impress, she was simply being kind. He dusted off his knee and sat down on the shawl, still holding the apple.

"You are an odd girl," he said, "what is your name?"

"Nyra, Your Majesty."

He took another bite, eyes narrowing with interest, "tell me, Nyra… why is it that everyone else cowers when I walk by, but you look at me like I am no more threatening than a stray dog?"

She tilted her head slightly, "why would I fear you? You are our king, not our enemy. You are here to protect us, not to do us harm." The King was quiet for a moment, letting her words settle. No one had ever spoken to him like that before. Her voice was gentle but firm, and honest in a way that almost disarmed him.

"You are an odd girl," the king repeated, "but you are honest and hold high values of modesty. I could use more people like you."

She was beautiful, but not in the polished way his court was used to. Her skin pale like the dead of winter, streaked with dirt, and her clothes ragged. But her eyes, crisp as ice, held something no one else's did. It was clear and unafraid. He stood and tossed the apple core aside.

"Take her," he said to the guards, "and the apples. Bring them both back to the castle."

There was a beat of hesitation, but no one dared question him. Two guards stepped forward and helped the girl to her feet, another collecting the barrel of apples. Nyra looked up at the King skeptically, but did not protest.

Two

The King's Attendant

As they arrived at the castle, Nyra glanced around, feeling like a smudge on a painted canvas. She followed the guards through towering iron gates, their hinges groaning open to reveal a world unlike anything she could have ever imagined. She had seen the castle from a distance, of course, its spires rising like stone fingers into the clouds, its banners fluttering proudly with the crest of Draymoor. But up close, it was something else entirely. The moment she stepped inside, the air itself changed. It was cooler, crisper, scented faintly with wax, wood polish, and floral incense.

Her boots echoed against polished marble floors that shimmered like water. Above her, the ceilings arched so high she half-expected stars to glitter from them. Walls of pale stone were traced with gold and etched with intricate carvings of hunting scenes, dragons, angels, kings with crowns too large for their heads. Everything sparkled. Chandeliers dripped crystals like frozen tears, catching the candlelight and throwing rainbows across the walls. The carpets were thick enough to bury your toes in, dyed in deep hues of crimson and royal blue. Columns lined the halls, each one unique. Some wrapped with vines carved into stone, others traced with tiles that shimmered like glass.

Nyra tried not to gape, but her eyes darted everywhere. A part of her wondered if she should be holding her breath, as if breathing wrong might shatter something. Even the light seemed different here, filtered through stained-glass windows that painted the floor with swirls of color. She could not imagine anyone actually living in a place like this. It did not feel real. It felt like walking through a painting she did not belong in. Yet here she was, trailing behind the guards, clutching the edge of her shawl like armor, leaving behind the dust and smoke of the village with every step. They passed through hallway after hallway, the maze of stone corridors and high archways blurring together until Nyra's head spun from trying to memorize every turn. Eventually, the guards stopped in front of a large wooden door. When it opened, a cloud of warmth and the scent of rose and lavender poured out. Inside, a group of maids waited.

"Clean her up and return her to me," King Corwin commanded, "dress her in the servant's uniform. She is to be my new personal attendant." He turned on his heel, guards falling into step behind him. Nyra blinked, stunned, as the door shut behind him.

One of the maids stepped forward with a kind smile, "hello, miss. I am Seren. You must be Nyra?"

"Yes," she replied softly, still a little overwhelmed, "how do you already know my name?"

Seren placed a hand on her shoulder to guide her to the bath, "word travels fast around the castle."

"What... exactly is going on? I am a little confused," Nyra's brow furrowed.

Seren let out a soft laugh, "from what we have heard, you have piqued the king's interest. You are going to be his personal attendant now. It is our job to get you court-ready."

"Me?" Nyra asked in disbelief, "**the King's attendant?**"

She nodded, "quite odd, I will admit. He has never chosen a commoner before. You must have made quite the impression." As Seren and the others bustled around, preparing the bath, steam began to curl through the air. It softened the candlelight, carrying sweet and unfamiliar fragrances of lavender, orange blossom, and something faintly spicy, like clove. The warmth kissed Nyra's cheeks, fogging the edge of the mirror and blurring the edges of the room around her.

She stood awkwardly as Seren approached with gentle hands, untying her worn shawl, "may I?" the maid asked softly, and Nyra nodded. Her voice was caught somewhere between nerves and awe. The layers of fabric were peeled away, revealing pale skin marked by work, and though she flushed under their gazes, there was no judgment in their eyes, only kindness. When she stepped into the bath, the heat embraced her like a summer hug, enveloping her limbs and chasing away the chill that had settled deep in her bones.

She let out a soft, involuntary sigh, her eyes fluttering shut. She had known only rivers, cold cloths, and the occasional cracked basin for bathing, never warmth like this, never a tub carved from polished marble and filled just for her.

"This water has been steeped with rose petals and milk," one maid explained gently, dipping a ladle and pouring it over Nyra's shoulders, "it is good for the skin."

Another began scrubbing her arms with a cloth, firm but careful, "you will feel like new, miss," she added with a smile.

The maids worked with practiced grace, lathering her hair in thick, creamy soap that foamed like clouds between their fingers. The scent of lemon balm and honey clung to the steam. Water streamed down her back in warm waves as they rinsed her clean, fingers threading through her tangled hair with patient care.

After the bath, they helped her into a robe so soft it felt like wearing air. They led her to a vanity, where the mirror reflected a different version of herself. A cleaner, calmer, and almost glowing girl. Her damp hair was combed and styled with elegant simplicity. No flashy ornaments, no heavy jewels. Just a small silver pin to sweep her hair from her face and a light touch of oil to bring out its shine.

"You have lovely features," Seren murmured, gently adjusting a strand of hair behind Nyra's ear, "no need to hide them."

Nyra blinked at her reflection, uncertain, "is this... really me?"

Seren smiled, "it has always been you. We are just helping you see it."

Then came the dress, a flowing garment of soft silk, dyed in muted tones, embroidered with patterns that shimmered faintly in the light. Her aura resembled a snowflake. A calming presence of nature that was unique to only her. It felt like wearing water. Nyra held her breath as they fastened it around her and slipped delicate shoes onto her feet. When they finally turned her toward the mirror, she stopped breathing altogether. The girl in the reflection was not a poor girl, scrapping for coins to survive. She was graceful, composed, royal, almost. It stirred memories of the times she had once been dressed for palace balls when she was a child musician. But even then, she had never looked like this. She turned slightly, watching the fabric swish around her legs. A smile stretched over her lips.

"So, what do you think?" Seren asked, eyes shining in a smile.

"I have never looked better," Nyra sighed, "you all did an incredible job."

Seren beamed, "then we mustn't keep the king waiting any longer."

With a final glance at the mirror and a small goodbye to the girl she used to be turning into the woman she was stepping into, Nyra followed Seren out of the room and down the long, winding halls toward the throne room.

Three

Glittering Snowfall

As they approached the throne room, the towering double doors, each carved with intricate scenes of past victories and royal lineage, swung open in perfect unison. The guards on either side stood motionless, their armor catching the light with a faint shimmer. Nyra hesitated for a moment, her heartbeat quickening. The throne room stretched out like a cathedral. Sunlight filtered through tall stained-glass windows, casting fragments of more color across the marble floor than Nyra ever thought existed.

Velvet banners in deep royal blue and crimson draped from the high arched ceiling, each one bearing the crest of House Draymoor: a golden falcon in flight above a ring of stars. Tapestries lined the stone walls with the long, solemn history of the throne she now approached. Every inch of the room shimmered with wealth. Nyra could hardly comprehend the cost of it all. The room alone was worth more than everything she and her family had ever owned... perhaps everything her entire village had owned for generations. The scale of it was both breathtaking and suffocating. She felt like a speck of dust inside a world built for gods.

At the far end of the chamber, King Corwin sat upon his throne. A towering seat of polished obsidian and gold, its armrests carved to resemble soaring falcons. He leaned slightly to one side, resting his chin on his knuckles as his eyes followed her closely. He smiled. The transformation had exceeded his expectations. Gone was the ragged girl from the village now standing before him was a vision of elegance. Her hair, freshly washed and gently styled, caught the light like a **glittering snowfall**. The simple lines of her dress only made her natural beauty more striking. She moved cautiously, her steps still unsure, but there was a quiet dignity to her posture. *How could someone like her have been hidden in plain sight?*

She did not know it, but she carried herself like a noblewoman. No, it was more than that. There was a softness to her, something untouched by pride or ambition. She had the face of a princess, yes, but the soul of someone real. And that, he thought, was rarer than any crown jewel. Nyra and Seren walked forward across the vast room and dropped to their knees before the throne. Nyra kept her eyes low, her palms pressed together tightly in her lap, trying to suppress the whirlwind of nerves. She could feel the physical weight of the king's gaze like a cloak made of stone.

"You did well Seren, you rarely disappoint," he praised her for her hard work.

She nodded in appreciation, "thank you, Your Majesty."

"Now leave us be. I wish to speak to Nyra alone," the king waved his hand and dismissed her. Seren stood up immediately, bowed, and then left the room, the doors shutting behind her. Now it was just Nyra and the King in the room. Her heartbeat picked up slightly at the unfamiliarity of this situation. Never in her life did she think she would be dressed in the finest clothes kneeling before the king himself alone in his throne room. It was an honor but a pressure she tried very hard not to let herself get crushed under.

"You may rise," the king said.

Nyra stood up slowly, "forgive me Your Majesty, I am a little confused."

"Confused? About what?" the king smiled.

"I was told you want me as your personal attendant. I am not sure why I was chosen. I have nothing to offer you, Your Majesty" she said.

The king chuckled, "perhaps not yet, but I can tell that you are going to add something special to this castle."

Nyra was still hesitant about the king wanting her in the castle but knew better to question him further, "Your Majesty, I have never been in the castle before, I do not know my way around. I doubt how well I can serve you."

Corwin rose from his throne in a fluid motion, his dark cloak trailing behind him like a shadow. The sharp sound of his boots striking the marble echoed through the silent hall. He descended down the platform with measured grace, stopping just in front of her. He looked down at her, his gaze steady, not cruel, but unreadable, as if studying a puzzle he intended to solve.

"Allow me to show you around," he said, voice smooth but edged with quiet command, "you seem like a smart girl. I am sure you will learn fast." The words were polite, but his tone left little room for refusal. He turned without waiting for a response, the heavy doors creaking open ahead of him as he moved toward them with purpose.

Nyra hesitated only a moment before trailing after him, her footsteps whispering softly against the polished floor. She kept a respectful distance, just as she had been taught. Close enough to follow, far enough not to offend.

The space between them felt thick with something unspoken. She could feel the weight of his presence even with his back to her, every movement precise, every step deliberate. She did not know what awaited her beyond those doors, but her heart beat faster as they passed through them together.

Four

Be Gentle With Beautiful Things

They walked in silence at first, the echo of their footsteps trailing behind them down long marble corridors. Corwin turned to Nyra as they strolled through a hall of polished stone arches and stained-glass windows, sunlight casting fractured rainbows across the floor.

"The castle may seem big and intimidating at first glance," he began, his tone warm but precise, "but I can assure you it is not as complex as it seems. Everything here has an order to it."

Nyra nodded silently, eyes wide as she tried to absorb both the king's words and the scenery around her. The hallway alone felt like a museum, the walls adorned with oil paintings of past monarchs. Stern-faced kings with golden eyes, women with jeweled crowns and soft expressions followed her where ever she went.

"The first floor," Corwin continued, "is the most open. Common areas, mostly halls for audiences, meeting rooms, open chambers where people gather. It is also where the public is sometimes allowed, such as in the courtyard. Though do not confuse it with the ballroom that lies on the third floor." Nyra tried to picture it all in her mind, mentally drawing a map she was not sure she would remember.

"The second floor is for the staff," he went on, "maids, stewards, cooks... Most of them work and live there. You will find the laundry, sewing rooms, and servant quarters. You will be staying in one of the eastern corridors on that level."

"That is... generous," Nyra thought. The idea of having her own room felt unreal.

Corwin smiled at her briefly, then continued, "the third floor is where most of the palace's more... elegant affairs take place. The ballroom, of course. the dining hall, connected to the kitchens. The royal library. You have already been to the throne room, but there is also a gallery next to it filled with heirlooms and war banners."

"And the fourth floor," Corwin said, his tone shifting lower and more guarded, "is off-limits to most. Very few are allowed there without permission. But *you*," he glanced over at her, "are an exception."

Her heart skipped slightly, "me?"

He nodded, "it is where my chambers are, along with rooms for guests to stay in. I will be showing you the route later when it is quieter. You will need to know it if you are to serve me directly. But there is also a room up there that you must *never* enter without me present. A sacred space. It is the chapel of the kings. Where portraits, relics, and the names of every past ruler are kept. Only the royal bloodline and the knights have access. Understood?"

Nyra nodded quickly, "yes, Your Majesty."

"The rest of the fourth floor is for armor and weaponry," he added with a dismissive wave of his hand, "that is of no concern to you. Someone else tends to all that."

She glanced at his profile as he walked beside her, strong, focused, but not cold. There was something very human about him, beneath all the polish and power. He spoke like a man who knew his duty well, but not without ignorance.

Corwin glanced at her again, "your role, Nyra, is simple. Stay near me unless I say otherwise. Be present. Be ready. You will attend to my needs, whether that means delivering messages, retrieving items, or simply listening when I need a voice I trust."

Nyra swallowed. The weight of it all began to settle into her chest, "I understand."

"If at any point you are lost, guards are stationed at nearly every corner. Do not hesitate to ask. It is better to ask than to wander." She nodded again, quietly thankful.

"You do not need to bother with the basement," he added, turning a corner and gesturing to a spiral staircase. "It is just wine barrels and the holding cells. Only my head guard and I have keys." Nyra instinctively shivered at the mention of cells.

"Outside," Corwin continued, "the west side of the castle holds the stables. The east is where knights train, sometimes there are tournaments. You may attend if I bring you with me. The south wall is where the woods begin. There is nothing of value out there for you."

Nyra opened her mouth to speak, but paused, "may I ask... Do you have many tournaments?"

He gave a soft laugh, "more than I would like. Knights love to prove their worth. Steel and pride make a tiring mix." Nyra smiled faintly.

Corwin stopped near a window overlooking the courtyard below, "it is a lot to take in, I know."

"Yes," she admitted quietly, "but I will do my best. I promise."

He turned to her, studying her for a beat longer than she expected, "I believe you will, Nyra," and then he gestured for her to follow once more, the echo of their footsteps continuing down the corridor. Nyra's eyes darted to every corner, the stained-glass windows casting jewel-toned reflections on the polished floors, the ornate gold-framed portraits of long-dead kings and queens lining the walls, the towering statues that stood like silent soldiers in every direction. Though the themes repeated throughout the castle, Nyra still could not get enough of the beauty.

"It is like a painting," she whispered.

Corwin glanced over his shoulder, "a cold one, I imagine."

Nyra blinked, "what do you mean?"

He slowed his steps slightly, "everything here is made to impress, to intimidate, to declare power. But it is not... warm," he gave a dry smile, "there is little comfort in perfection."

Nyra hesitated before replying, "I have never had perfection, so it feels... magical to me," she stopped at a large archway and peeked into the room beyond, "that chandelier must be made of real crystal."

"It is," Corwin said, "the craftsman was paid in land. He retired wealthier than most noblemen."

She gave a soft laugh, "for one chandelier?"

Corwin turned to face her, "value is relative. What might feed your village for years might be nothing but decoration here."

Nyra looked at the king and the way he carried himself as he walked. It was clear that these values of perfection and modesty were embedded into him from a young age. She suddenly became conscious of her own sloppiness. Even if she was dressed like a noblewoman she still had the unconscious mannerisms of a commoner, "I do not belong in a place like this."

He stepped closer, "you do now." Nyra doubted his certainty. She looked up at him, searching for insincerity, but found only calm conviction in his expression. They continued walking. Corwin led Nyra through the courtyard garden. The fragrance of roses was thick in the air as they passed clusters of blooms arranged in careful symmetry around the white marble fountain. Nyra slowed her steps, her fingers grazing the soft petals, tracing their edges as delicate as snowfall.

"I used to steal rose petals as a child," she said quietly, her voice softening as if lost in memory, "my mother would dry them, sew them into our pillowcases so they would smell sweet."

Corwin's gaze lingered on her, a slight flicker of intrigue in his eyes, "that is clever."

"It was all we had," Nyra murmured, her fingers brushing the petals once more, "we did not have much, so we had to make what we could feel beautiful." For a moment, silence fell between them. The only sound was the gentle rustling of leaves, the soft murmur of water from the fountain.

"You speak differently than the others here," Corwin said, his tone contemplative, "you do not try to impress me, not like the others. It is... refreshing."

Nyra met his eyes, a glint of amusement dancing in hers, "I do not know how to impress a king," she said, the faintest curve of a smile on her lips.

"That is probably why you did," Corwin replied, stepping a bit closer, his hand lightly brushing against one of the roses. His voice had a note of something unspoken, a shift that lingered in the air between them. Nyra's heart skipped, her cheeks flushed with a sudden warmth. She quickly looked away, pretending to study the twisting vine that clung to the side of a column. The subtle tension between them hung like a fragile thread.

Corwin watched her for a moment, his gaze lingering longer than before, his thoughts unreadable, "there is a certain... calm about you, Nyra," he said, his voice quieter now, almost as if he were speaking to himself, "even in a world full of chaos, you seem to find peace."

She glanced back at him, her expression softening, "perhaps that is because I have always known chaos. In my life, peace was never something I expected, but something I had to make."

Corwin's gaze softened, something between admiration and a flicker of something unexpected, "you are unlike anyone I have ever known."

"So are you," Nyra smiled, "I never expected a king to be so... gentle."

"My mother taught me to **be gentle with beautiful things**," Corwin let his finger gracefully glide over the petals. Nyra's breath caught in her throat. Her heart began to race, but she refused to let it show. She turned her focus back to the garden, her fingers tightening around the vine as if she was anchoring herself.

Seren returned quietly, her steps light across the stone as she approached the king and Nyra. She bowed before Corwin, "Your Majesty, Elowyn asked me to inform you that your lunch is ready."

"Thank you, Seren. Inform her I will be there shortly," Corwin said, his voice courteous, though his attention had already begun to drift elsewhere. His tone was not unkind, but it was dismissive, almost distant. Nyra noticed the way he treated Seren with respect, yet kept her at arm's length. She wondered if there was history there she had not yet seen. Seren bowed again and disappeared down the corridor in a swirl of dark skirts. Corwin withdrew his hand from the rose and began to walk toward the archway leading out of the courtyard. Nyra followed quickly, falling into step behind him. The warmth of the sun faded as they moved back into the cool stone halls of the castle.

Five

Secret Family Recipe

As they made their way up toward the dining hall, Nyra spoke, her tone polite but tinged with curiosity, "Your Majesty, if I may ask... I am curious about something."

"Go ahead," Corwin replied, eyes forward, his voice calm.

"How did Seren become one of your maids?"

He paused mid-step, just a brief pause in his stride, before continuing, "she is my mother's former husband's daughter," he said, "after her parents passed, my mother took her in. Even though they were not blood, she felt it was the right thing to do. That lasted until she married my father. He was not fond of Seren, and he cast her out." Nyra frowned faintly, sadness creeping into her expression.

"When I became king, I thought she deserved better," Corwin went on, "I invited her back. She was bitter toward me, said things to me that my father would have had her executed for," he let out a short, humorless breath, "but in some way, she was family. So I asked again and again, until she finally returned."

Nyra listened carefully, the story adding quiet weight to her growing understanding of him. He was a king, yes, but not without conscience. There was empathy beneath the crown.

"She prefers solitude now," Corwin added, "and I respect that. I keep our interactions brief not out of rudeness, but to honor her space, and avoid stirring the ashes of old anger."

Nyra absorbed it in silence. The explanation was sad, but it painted Corwin in a new light, a man trying to mend wounds he did not create. They walked on, the corridor stretching ahead in quiet elegance, their footsteps softened by thick carpet and flickering torchlight. She stole a glance at him, wondering what kind of weight he carried behind that calm exterior.

Just as she opened her mouth to speak, the guards ahead pushed open a set of towering doors. The scent of various foods and spiced wine drifted out to meet them. As they stepped inside, Nyra's breath caught.

A long table stretched across the room, gleaming with polished silver and shining goblets. Dozens of dishes lined its surface. Roasted meats, golden pastries, bowls of steaming vegetables, and pitchers of spiced wine. It was more food than Nyra had seen in her entire life, let alone at a single meal.

Corwin took his seat at the head of the table and gestured to the chair beside him, "sit," he said. Nyra hesitated, startled. He did not mean for *her* to sit there, did he? She glanced at him, uncertain. Corwin chuckled, reading her expression, "do not just stare at it, grab some food."

She moved carefully to the chair, her movements gentle, as though the moment might shatter if she did anything too suddenly. Her eyes fell on her empty plate as though it did not belong to her. "Is all of this made just for you?" she asked softly.

Corwin laughed again, shaking his head as he poured himself a glass of wine, "do I look like I could eat all this alone? There is an order to things. I eat first along with any guests or my attendant. Then the knights, the guards, the maids and servants, and finally the kitchen staff."

Nyra tilted her head, her brows furrowing, "but... what if the food runs out before the kitchen staff eats?"

"That is why they are last," he explained, "if there is nothing left, they are allowed to prepare whatever they need for themselves. They always eat," he glanced at her untouched plate and smirked, "come on. I know you have hands. Eat."

Nyra picked up a fork and reached for the nearest platter, something roasted and spiced, the aroma rich and inviting. She took a bite, and her eyes widened. It was unlike anything she had ever tasted, so tender and warm, layered with flavor that lingered on her tongue. She took another bite, then another, and then reached for something else. A crisp pastry, a roasted root vegetable, a slice of sweet melon. Her senses swam with delight.

Corwin watched her, his expression softening. At first, he was amused by her enthusiasm, the way she seemed to forget herself in the moment. But then, something else settled in his chest. Her joy was simple, unmasked, and in a world where everyone wore carefully selected expressions and spoke with gilded tongues, her sincerity felt like sunlight breaking through a dense fog.

He found himself leaning in ever so slightly, drawn by the brightness in her eyes, the subtle hum of happiness she radiated. It reminded him of how life must have felt before he was crowned, before the weight of the throne dulled his senses, before every word and glance was measured.

She laughed softly when she bit into the melon, surprised by its sweetness, and the sound struck him like a melody he had not heard in years. He smiled, not the kind he wore for courtiers and councilmen, but something quieter and real.

He looked away, reaching for his own goblet as if the wine might cool the warmth that had crept into his veins. He was a king. She was a servant. This, whatever this was, should not be. And yet, for a few stolen seconds, he let himself watch her again, his smile returning despite himself.

As she tried another dish, a memory struck her, "Your Majesty... were my apples brought here with me?"

He nodded, "they were sent to the kitchen."

"I wonder... Do your cooks know how to use them properly? That variety does not grow around here, does it?"

"They are familiar with foreign foods. We have guests and traders bring unusual things often. But their knowledge is more limited when it comes to rare produce," he said, "why? Do you have some **secret family recipe**?"

"A few, actually," Nyra smiled, "they are not secrets, though. I would be happy to share them. Especially now... with all these ingredients and spices, I imagine they could taste even better than they ever did back home."

Corwin's eyes lit up with interest, "please do. Write them down when you have time. I would love to give your recipes a home in my kitchen."

She nodded, slowly at first, then with more certainty, "I will," she said, her voice soft but steady. A strange warmth spread through her chest with pride. Not the kind born of vanity, but the quiet kind that came from being seen. A servant's skills were usually invisible, absorbed into the machinery of the castle and forgotten. But here, at this table, the king had looked at her and said *your voice matters*.

When Corwin finally stood, he turned to her again, "are you ready to see the rest of the castle?"

Nyra rose with him, a flicker of excitement brightening her eyes. She was liking her time in the castle even if she was just a mere servant, "yes, Your Majesty."

Six

Cedric Draymoor

Nyra could not stop herself from glancing at him when she thought he would not notice. He was not what she expected. There was a thoughtfulness in the way he spoke, and loneliness behind his confident posture.

She found herself wondering how much of his day was spent in silence, how many of his decisions were made without anyone truly knowing the man behind the crown. His steps were steady, purposeful, but the air around him seemed quieter than it should be for someone constantly surrounded by people.

As they reached a large arched window that overlooked the eastern courtyard, he paused, placing a hand on the cool stone of the frame. Below, knights sparred in the practice yard, their movements sharp and disciplined.

"I used to train with them more often," Corwin said, his gaze distant, "before the council insisted I focus more on diplomacy and appearances."

Nyra stood beside him, glancing from the yard to his face, "do you miss it?"

"Sometimes it is easier to know who you are with a sword in your hand. It is simpler, out there, you know your enemy. In here…" he gestured to the castle around them, "...they smile with daggers behind their back."

She hesitated, then said softly, "a sword makes you strong, but it can not protect you from silence, betrayal, or loneliness."

He turned his head slowly to look at her, and for a moment, the veil slipped. The king was still there, but beneath him, the man emerged. A man who carried burdens no one ever asked if he wanted. A man who had learned to guard his heart with armor finer than steel.

"How is it that you always say the one thing I was trying not to admit to myself?"

She did not reply, but her silence felt thoughtful, not uncomfortable. He looked at her then, catching her watching him. Nyra did not mean to touch anything so tender, but now it was open between them. The wind stirred her skirts and blew a lock of her hair, and before she could reach for it, Corwin lifted his hand. His fingers brushed the strand gently behind her ear, and for one suspended moment, the world felt still. No courtiers. No guards. No thrones or duties or names. Just two people on a balcony, looking at each other like they had never really seen anyone before.

Nyra did not pull away from him. His closeness, the warmth of his fingers near her skin, was oddly comforting and intimate in a way that felt both impossible and undeniable. Her breath was shallow, caught somewhere between fear and something far softer.

For a heartbeat, neither moved. The air between them hummed, thick with the weight of what remained unsaid. Then the sharp clatter of swords from below rang out like a bell, shattering the stillness. Corwin's eyes flicked back to the yard, the spell broken. He drew in a quiet breath and straightened, the subtle shift in his posture pulling the distance back between them. But the silence that followed was not empty. Something had shifted quietly and permanently. And though the moment had passed, it left a trace in its wake, like the fading warmth of a hand just released.

"You are not afraid of me," he said, almost amused.

Nyra blinked, "should I be?"

"I do not know," he admitted, "most people are, at least a little. They see the crown before they see the man."

"I see both," she said softly, "but I do not think either frighten me."

For a moment, the hallway stilled. His expression changed, faint surprise, followed by a quieter gesture. Appreciation, maybe. Then he smiled again, "you speak with honesty, Nyra. That is rare in this place."

"I do not know how to be anything else," she replied, "lying to royalty never ends well, or so I have been told."

He laughed, low and warm, "you are not wrong."

They resumed walking, his pace slower now, as though he did not mind taking longer with her. As they passed through a set of tall gilded doors, the scent of parchment and aged wood surrounded them. The royal archives. Scrolls and books filled countless drawers.

Nyra stared in wonder, "have you read all of these?"

"I have tried," he said, "but I do not have the time I once did. My father believed knowledge was a king's best weapon. He would lock me in here for hours when I was younger. At the time I thought it was punishment."

"And now?"

He looked around the room, then back at her, "now I wish I had more hours to be locked in."

It was a strange feeling, walking side by side with a king, seeing the cracks in his armor, hearing the softness in his voice. He was not just a ruler. He was a man who had grown up in a gilded cage, learning how to wear its bars like a crown.

"Come," he said at last, "there is still one more place I want to show you." They walked up a narrow stairway, quieter than the rest of the castle, where the footsteps echoed against the stone. At the top of the stairs was a heavy oak door carved with the crests of the past kings. Corwin pulled a small silver key from his pocket and turned it in the lock.

"This room is sacred. It is reserved for the memory of those who came before me," he pushed the door open, revealing a small chapel bathed in soft golden light. Tall windows let the sun pour in, illuminating stained-glass depictions of kings and queens long gone. Candles flickered along the edges of the room, their scent faintly herbal, calming. In the center was a simple altar of stone, carved with ancient words Nyra could not read. She stepped in slowly, the aura of the space settling over her like a quiet hush.

Corwin did not speak for a while. When he did, his voice was quiet, almost a whisper, "when I was crowned, I came here every night for a week. I did not know what I was doing. I still do not, not really. But I needed to feel like I was not alone in it."

Nyra looked up at him, "and do you still come here?"

He nodded once, "when I need to remember who I am."

As Corwin moved to open the heavy curtains, golden light spilled slowly into the chapel, unveiling the quiet sight within the back of the chapel. The illumination danced across the polished stone floor and lit up the forgotten corners of the room, casting a glow on the treasures held within, aged armor, ancient scrolls in glass cases, and weathered relics from kings long past.

But what captured Nyra's attention was the massive painting that dominated the far wall. It had to be at least a hundred feet tall, stretching from floor to vaulted ceiling. Her breath caught in her throat as she stepped closer, awe widening her eyes. She could hardly fathom how something so enormous had been painted at all, let alone with such stunning detail. The man in the painting stood tall and imposing, with a crown upon his head and a sword resting against his shoulder. His eyes, dark and commanding, seemed to follow her no matter where she moved.

Corwin chuckled softly behind her, "that is **Cedric Draymoor**, the founder of this kingdom." Nyra remained transfixed. Cedric looked every bit the legend she had grown up hearing about. The fierce, regal, and hauntingly handsome king that started the history of the Draymoor kingdom. But no story had ever prepared her for this. Staring up too long made her dizzy. The scale was disorienting, like staring up at the sky and feeling like you might fall into it. She took a step back to steady herself and bumped right into Corwin. He caught her with quick hands, gently guiding her back to her feet. She blinked, startled, as her balance returned. His grip was firm but careful, his expression amused as he looked down at her.

Nyra's cheeks flushed with embarrassment, "I am sorry, I did not expect it to feel so… enormous."

"It is," Corwin said, still smiling, "you are not the first to nearly tip over from looking at it too long." She averted her eyes from the painting, not trusting herself to stare at it again just yet. His hand remained on her arm, warm and grounding.

"My mother used to tell me Cedric Draymoor fought a pack of giants to win this land," Corwin said, his voice quieting with memory, "and that he befriended one of them, a gentle one who painted that for him as a gift."

Nyra looked at him and laughed, "giants?"

He shrugged slightly, his eyes on the painting now, "it was just one of her bedtime stories. I think she made it up to help me sleep. But I liked believing it." There was a softness to him as he spoke that caught Nyra off guard. A boyish fondness in place of his usual royal pride. The air between them shifted, as if time had slowed just enough for the moment to stretch. They stood there together, surrounded by silence and memory. And in that moment, the distance between king and commoner felt like it did not matter. Nyra's heart fluttered. She did not dare move.

Corwin blinked, realizing the quiet had lingered too long. He cleared his throat, gently releasing her arm and stepping back, "as I mentioned before," he said, tone more formal now, "this room is sacred. It is restricted to the royal lineage and the knights alone. You are permitted here only when I say so. Understand?"

Nyra nodded quickly, the echo of his touch still tingling on her skin, "yes, Your Majesty." Without another word, they exited the chapel, stepping back into the corridor where sunlight seemed just a bit too bright after the quiet intimacy they had shared.

As they descended the stairwell, Nyra's heart remained lodged in her throat. There was something about the king that unsettled her in a way that was not unpleasant. His unexpected humanity, the humility threaded through his powerful presence. It was unlike anything she had known. She tried to suppress the thoughts stirring within her. A servant had no business feeling this way about a man of such status, especially the king.

Seven

Silk on Glass

Back on the third floor, her mind shifted focus. She recalled every hallway and room they had passed, mentally tracing the castle's layout, trying to commit it all to memory.

Lifting her gaze to Corwin, she asked, "Your Majesty, what about the ballroom?" The word stirred something within her, nostalgia, maybe. Ballrooms had once played a large part in her past.

Corwin glanced at her, seeming momentarily dismissive, "it is located just beyond the dining hall."

"May I see it?" she asked, a soft urgency in her tone.

He raised an eyebrow, intrigued, "why? It is nothing more than a large, empty room."

"I have spent a lot of time in ballrooms before. I am just... curious," she replied, her voice gentle but honest.

He paused, clearly weighing her words, then nodded, "very well. This way," and with that, he turned and began walking. Nyra followed, her pulse quickening from the anticipation of seeing the ballroom.

Once they stepped inside, Nyra was breathless. She had seen many elegant ballrooms before, but none came close to this one. It was massive and grander than anything she had ever imagined. The ceiling soared high above, its surface covered in a mural that seemed to tell a story across time. Nyra could have stood there for hours, studying the brushstrokes that expressed much life. Sunlight poured in from the towering windows, casting the room in a warm glow. The late afternoon painted everything in rich tones of amber and gold, as if the very walls were kissed by fire. Then she saw it... the piano. Tucked into a corner, its glossy black surface stood in stark contrast to the brightness of the room. Her heart skipped. Her breath caught. The sight of it sent a shiver through her fingertips.

Memories she had buried deep surged to the surface. Echoes of music, of childhood, of things once loved and lost. Corwin noticed her shift immediately. Her silence, her stillness. He scanned the room, puzzled, wondering what she was seeing that he was not.

"Your Majesty..." Nyra's voice was a whisper, fragile and trembling, "may I... may I play the piano?"

Corwin raised a brow, surprised, "you can play?"

Nyra scoffed a sort of laugh, "I used to..."

He nodded without hesitation, "of course. Go ahead."

Her legs felt weak as she moved. She approached the piano like it might vanish if she stepped too quickly. Trembling hands reached for the small bench, pulling it out gently before lowering herself onto it. Every movement was deliberate. She lifted the lid slowly, her hands hovering over the keys. She did not play right away, just let her fingers rest on the cool ivory, breathing in deeply. Then, eyes closed, she pressed down a simple chord.

The sound rang out, rich and full, echoing through the vaulted room like a voice awakened from slumber. Nyra's head spun with the memory. She saw herself again, small hands on worn keys, the scent of the expensive perfumes in the air, the faint laughter of a life far away.

Behind her, Corwin leaned against the wall, arms folded. He watched her closely. There was a haunting fragileness in the way she moved. He heard the note she played and it stirred something in him too. A memory. His mother's voice. The music that used to flood this room during her lavish parties. The ballroom alive with light and song. That single note, drawn from the past, hung between them, binding two very different lives with the shared thread of something they once cherished.

Nyra pressed down another chord, slow and thoughtful, as if she were testing the piano's soul. Then, taking in a steady breath, she placed both hands gently on the keys. Her eyes fluttered shut, surrendering to the muscle memory buried deep within her. And then she played. Her fingers moved with delicate precision, gliding over the keys like **silk on glass**. The music poured from her in a tender, aching melody, like a voice calling out from the depths of her heart, reaching back through time. It was not just a song; it was a quiet attempt to soothe, to heal some unseen wound.

Nyra's heart ached with a reborn love and a throbbing reminder of the past. She reminisced about the evenings after dinner when she would run to the old woman next door. The gentle soul who welcomed her with a smile, loving her like a daughter. The woman would pull out the bench from under the piano, inviting her to a whole new world. Nyra would sit beside the aged woman and let her heart rest and heal after the weight of each day.

Her love for the creation of symphonic melodies is the only thing she had to hold on to. She was not strong. She was not clever. She could not cook. She was as clumsy as a newborn foal. Nyra was useless except for the fact that she could make *music*. After her parents fell ill and she had become the caretaker in the family, she was forced to use her only skill.

Working as the pianist at the southern palace balls of the Ignas Kingdom turned her blessing into a curse. The keys no longer felt like freedom, but chains. It became the shackles that held her hands to the piano against her will. Music was no longer an escape from the troubling life of a peasant, but a prison. Playing until her mind went numb, her hands weak and cramping. If at any point she missed a note or fumbled a rhythm, the Noble's cane reminded her of the cost. Pain in exchange for perfection.

But here, now, she sat on the bench once again. Not playing nobles. Not for coins. Not for survival. She was playing for herself. Letting her mind go quiet for the first time in years. Letting her past heal into the future. Nyra smiled as the sound filled the room.

Corwin stood transfixed. He had heard music before, grand orchestras, masterful performers, but nothing like this. Nothing that felt so alive. The way Nyra sat at the piano, the way her body moved with the instrument, it was as though she was not playing it at all, but the piano was playing her. She was like snow. Fragile in appearance, but impossible to ignore. And just like snow, she made the world feel quieter when she entered it. Drawing the truth from her bones, the sorrow from her soul, the love from her heart. He could hear it in every note. A quiet grief. A trace of regret. A mourning for something lost. But underneath it all was a radiant light. A stubborn flicker of hope. It took his breath away.

The final note rang out like a whisper, trembling through the air before fading into silence. Nyra ran her hand down the keys one last time, as if saying goodbye. She held it there, suspended, until even the echo dissolved, and the room was still once more, holding the memory of music like a held breath.

"You are incredible," was all Corwin could manage to say. Yes, she was incredible, but she was also something more. The words he needed to express that simply would not come.

Nyra gave a soft, faint smile, "thank you. I was nervous, I have not played in years."

"Where did you learn to play like that?" he asked, still stunned.

"My neighbor, a sweet old woman, taught me," she replied, her smile faltering slightly, "I used to perform at balls and galas at the South Palace in the Ignas Kingdom when I was younger. My parents fell deathly ill, and I had to earn money by doing the only thing I knew how to do. I played from the beginning of those dances to the end."

Corwin's expression darkened with disbelief, "from start to finish? Those events can go on from sunrise to sunset, or longer..."

Nyra nodded solemnly, "it was the only way I could keep my family alive. I once played for nearly six days straight with barely any rest. My hands went numb. My fingers started bleeding. They fired me after that for damaging their precious piano." She looked down at her fingertips, slightly misshapen, calloused, worn from years of sacrifice.

Corwin's eyes softened, "you gave everything you had... for your family."

"A sacrifice made for nothing," she whispered, her voice low but piercing through the room like a blade.

His heart caught in his throat, "what do you mean?"

Nyra inhaled slowly, her shoulders heavy with the weight of memory, "my parents were sick. My sister was too young to work, so she stayed home and took care of them while I earned what little I could. That night, after I was fired, I came home to find them all huddled by the fire, dead. My sister contracted the disease from our parents and died with them. I was gone for too long to prevent that from happening. My sister, such a dumb little girl, refused to leave their side no matter how dangerous I told her it was..." her voice trembled, but she pressed on, "I lost everything that night. My family, my job... my love for music. It felt like my soul had been stripped from my body."

Corwin stood frozen in place, heart aching as he watched the light dim in her eyes. Her head was bowed, as if the weight of her grief were too much to bear, "you did not have a doctor to care for them?" he asked softly, "why did your sister have to do it alone?"

Nyra slowly raised her gaze, tears slipping down her cheeks, "Your Majesty, people like me do not have the luxury of doctors. I barely made enough to feed us. Medical care was out of reach." The truth struck him harder than any blade. He had always known life outside the castle walls was harder, but not like this. Not in the way Nyra described: raw, helpless, and cruel.

Now, standing in the golden ballroom of his ancestors, Corwin realized that while his world was blessed in silk and gold, hers had been built on blood and broken keys. Yet, here she stood, still whole, still kind, still willing to give. Somehow, that broke him more than anything. Corwin let his guard fall, just for a moment. The weight of her story, her pain, her strength, it was too much to carry in silence. He slowly sat beside her on the bench, their shoulders lightly touching, and gently took her hand in his.

"I will summon doctors from across the land," he said, voice low but firm, "they will be here always available to anyone who needs them. I know it will not bring back your family... but perhaps it can prevent others from suffering the same fate."

Nyra gave a faint, weary smile, "that is very generous of you,"

Corwin's pride as king slipped, quiet and unceremonious, as he continued to hold her hand. His gaze found hers, and in it was something rare, almost like an apology, "my ignorance blinded me," he confessed, "I sit on a throne surrounded by gold, while people are dying in silence just beyond the gates. If I had known... God, if I had only known, I would have acted sooner." His breath caught. He had never said anything like this to anyone. Never allowed himself to feel so *small*, so unsure. "I know it may be hard to believe, but I do care. I *do*. I want to help... I just do not know how."

Nyra squeezed his hand, "listen," she said.

Corwin blinked, "listen to what?"

She looked at him then, and something in her gaze rooted him to the floor, "the people," she answered simply, "if you truly care for them... listen to them." Her words were not dressed in grand language, but they struck him harder than any noble speech ever had. They held no demand, only truth. And Corwin felt it like a ripple through his bones. This dawning realization that maybe being a great king was not about strength or strategy. Maybe it started with listening.

He stared down at their joined hands, his thumb brushing across her calloused knuckles. "I will," he said softly, "I swear it." They lingered in silence a moment longer, hands still joined, the weight of everything unspoken pressing gently between them.

Corwin was the first to move. He stood, reluctantly releasing her hand, and cleared his throat, "you will need time to prepare for dinner," he said, his voice softer now, touched by something deeper, "let me show you to your chambers." Nyra nodded quietly, getting up from the bench. Her fingertips still tingled from the piano.

Eight

Protect the People Who Can Not Protect Themselves

The walk back through the castle was quieter than before. A different kind of tension hung in the air, not uncomfortable, but fragile, like the hush after a storm. They reached a long corridor lined with tall windows and oil paintings, the golden light of late afternoon spilling across the floor like melted honey.

Corwin stopped at a door near the end of the hallway. It was carved with delicate vines and roses, "this room is yours now," he said, opening the door for her. Nyra stepped inside, her breath catching. The room was spacious and elegant, with soft cream walls, a canopied bed, and a tall wardrobe carved from rich oak. Sunlight filtered in through lace curtains, painting patterns on the floor. A small vanity stood near the window, and on the desk beside it, a vase of fresh roses had already been placed.

"All this for a servant?" she asked, turning to face him.

Corwin looked at her, the corners of his mouth lifting in a faint smile, "yes, everyone who works here deserves comfort and warmth here in the castle. If there is anything you need, just let someone know. Dinner will be at dusk."

Nyra nodded again, unsure of what to say. The king hesitated, like he wanted to say something more, but instead, he offered her one last glance, then turned and walked away, the soft click of the door closing behind him leaving her alone in the room.

For a moment, she simply stood there, hands clasped in front of her, staring at the space around her. She had a room. A room of her own. A bed with sheets that looked softer than clouds, a wardrobe she had not dared dream of. The sunlight somehow felt warmer and gentler. She walked to the window and placed her hand on the glass, looking out across the gardens. For the first time in years, she felt... still.

She moved to the wardrobe, running her fingers over the polished wood before opening it. Inside hung several gowns of rich fabrics in many colors, clearly chosen with care. She found a soft white one that shimmered faintly in the light, and lifted it from its hanger.

As Nyra changed, her mind wandered to her family, to the piano, to Corwin's eyes as he had looked at her on that bench. For the first time since she had stepped into the castle, she allowed herself a small moment of hope that maybe she could stop fighting for survival and finally *live*.

Corwin stood outside Nyra's door longer than he should have. The quiet click of it closing between them had not dulled the sound of her voice echoing in his mind.

"Listen to them."

Such simple words. Spoken with no intention to hurt, but they had cut through him all the same. He turned and walked away, his pace slower than usual. He passed the marble columns and arched windows of the east wing with eyes that did not really see them. He had walked these halls his entire life, he knew every crack in the floor, every change in the light, but today, they felt different. The council room awaited him. It always did.

Inside, Lord Halwin unrolled a parchment with his usual stiff efficiency, "the outer provinces are requesting additional provisions for the coming winter. Grain stores have dropped, and livestock numbers are–" but Corwin was not listening. Not really. His gaze was fixed on the flicker of candlelight reflecting off the polished table. His thoughts were in a quiet village house where a young girl once played piano to keep her family alive. A girl who bled through her music until her body gave out, and still...*still*, was thrown away like she meant nothing. And he had never known. None of it. How many others were like her? Quietly breaking beneath the weight of survival while he sat in gold-trimmed rooms deciding how many barrels of wheat were "sufficient"? He had believed his intentions were enough, that because he wanted to be a good king, he was one. But that was not how it worked, was it? Wanting to help was not the same as doing it.

He interrupted without thinking, "Lord Halwin, when was the last time we sent healers to the outer villages?"

Halwin blinked, caught off guard, "healers, sire? I– well, they are dispatched during outbreaks or urgent needs, but regular visits? That is not the current protocol."

Corwin frowned, "why not?"

Halwin hesitated, "because, Your Majesty... we do not have the resources. Not consistently. And there have not been any formal requests for–"

"No one requests what they have never been given permission to hope for," Corwin said quietly, more to himself than to the lord. A silence fell between them.

Corwin stood abruptly, "we will continue this tomorrow."

"Sire?"

"Tomorrow," he repeated, already heading for the door. He needed air.

As he stepped out onto the balcony, the cool wind met his face and ruffled his hair. The sun was lowering itself gently behind the hills, casting long gold shadows across the courtyard. And somewhere inside, Nyra was getting ready for dinner. Alone, in a strange room, after spilling the story of her heartbreak to a king. He had never felt more like a boy pretending to wear a crown. He gripped the railing, the stone cool beneath his fingers.

You are the king. Fix it.

But it did not feel that simple anymore. Nyra had shown him what suffering looked like without ever meaning to. She had offered him truth, unvarnished and raw, and asked nothing in return. Somehow, that honest ache had shaken the very foundation of everything he thought he knew about justice, about service, about his people.

He had always ruled from a distance, protected by velvet and title and protocol. But now, distance felt like cowardice. And the girl with the bruised hands and soft, grieving eyes had become the lens through which he saw his kingdom more clearly than ever before.

Corwin had lost track of time. The light outside had shifted to deep amber, and a servant's distant bell reminded him it was time for dinner. Tonight was meant to be special. A formal gathering of knights and noblemen from across his own kingdom and neighboring realms. A show of strength and diplomacy. The kind of evening he once might have enjoyed. But now, after Nyra there was a pit in his stomach, an aching, shameful weight that refused to settle. The idea of dining among the rich and comfortable, while people like Nyra bled themselves dry for scraps, made his skin crawl. *How could this be the order of the world? How had he let it become this way?*

His mother's voice came back to him, gentle but firm, *"you must grow strong to* **protect the people who can not protect themselves,** *Corwin."* She used to whisper that as he cried in her lap after palace tutors punished him for soft-heartedness. She never tried to harden him. She taught him that strength and compassion could live in the same soul. What would she think of him now?

Nine

Why a Commoner, Corwin?

He reached the doors of the dining hall, hesitating for a breath. The sound of laughter and clinking glasses spilled out. Then, with quiet breath, he pushed the doors open and stepped into the room. The long banquet table stretched before him, heavy with silver platters and gold-rimmed plates. The warm glow of chandeliers shimmered off polished armor and embroidered sleeves. And there at the far end was Nyra.

She wore the white gown once owned by his mother's personal attendant, and in it, she looked like something out of a memory he had not known he was still carrying. The soft fabric caught the candlelight, and the way she moved with measured, graceful, poise without even trying, echoed the quiet dignity of another era. She held a bottle of wine with steady hands, offering each guest a gentle courtesy as she filled their goblets. The noblemen watched her with pleasant amusement, some a bit too intently, their laughter loud and careless. Corwin's gaze did not waver.

That dress brought him back to the days before the crown had grown so heavy. To evenings when his mother still hosted feasts in this very hall, her laughter trailing through the corridors like music. Her attendants had always moved like shadows of her grace, elegant, precise, and trusted. He remembered one in particular: kind eyes, a warm presence, a quiet strength that had soothed him during his most restless boyhood nights.

Now, watching Nyra, that memory stirred again, like dust rising from a sunlit floor. The nostalgia wrapped around him, soft and bittersweet. Not because she reminded him of the attendant exactly, but because she seemed to belong to that same world of the gentle, grounded, and untouched by the ambition that clung to everyone else in the room.

Her eyes lifted and met his, and for a breath, the hall dimmed. She offered a small, shy smile. Not calculated or rehearsed, just real. And Corwin, with the echo of memory still tugging at the edges of his chest, returned it, warm, sincere and a little too long

"Ah, Corwin, you have come at last," called an all too familiar voice. Darion. He sat at the other end of the table, one hand lazily cradling his wine glass, the other draped over the arm of his chair. His smirk held a sharpness that Corwin had grown wary of.

They had been close once. A bond only brothers could share. But after the suggestion that Darion might one day inherit the throne because Corwin did not possess an heir, something had shifted. Power tasted too sweet on Darion's tongue. He acted like a king now without the burden of earning it.

Nyra quickly stepped forward, pulling out Corwin's chair with a quiet smile. He sat down, nodding his thanks, touched again by the effortless way she cared for others. She had not been trained for this life. Yet she moved through it with grace.

"You have found yourself a lovely attendant, Your Majesty," a young knight from the western border said with a crooked smile, his eyes lingering too long on Nyra. Corwin's jaw tightened.

"She is lovely," Darion added, swirling his wine, "but I am curious... **Why a *commoner*, Corwin?** You have always selected ladies of noble birth. As did our father. His father before him. What makes *this* girl so special?" Nyra stood beside him, straight-backed, but Corwin saw the slight tension in her shoulders. She did not speak, though the room seemed to press in on her.

Corwin turned to Darion, his voice even but cold, "I have my reasons."

Darion's brows lifted with false innocence. "Oh, I am sure you do. But you must admit it is *unusual*. Untraditional, even. People will ask questions. They already are. An attendant is supposed to be someone you can trust. How can you trust a peasant?"

Corwin's eyes narrowed, "they will receive the same answer. I am the king. She fulfills her duties with excellence. That is all that matters." The finality in his voice cut through the murmurs like a blade. Darion leaned back, feigning indifference as he sipped his wine, though Corwin could see the displeasure setting in his jaw.

Dinner moved forward, but the food tasted like ash in Corwin's mouth. They spoke of military strategies, of shifting borders, of the gold imports from the northern trade lines. He heard the words, nodded at the right moments, but his mind drifted. This all felt hollow and predictable. These were the same discussions, repeated with different faces, year after year. They spoke of war like a board game, of peasants like numbers on a parchment. Not one of them had ever asked *what happened to the girl after the music stopped?*

Nyra had asked questions, hard and honest ones. She had offered him more perspective in a single day than half his council had given in years. Her thoughts were refreshing and untainted by greed or tradition. She challenged his beliefs simply by existing. Corwin found himself wondering: *What if leadership was not about tradition at all? What if it was about listening? About humility? About finding voices like Nyra's and letting them be heard?*

He looked up, catching her from across the table as she gently set a full goblet before a graying knight. She glanced at Corwin just once, then moved on. She never interrupted, never tried to insert herself, but somehow, her presence shaped the air of the room.

The evening wore on, laughter growing louder and the wine flowing like water. But Corwin had stopped laughing long ago. The young knight from the western border had taken a particular interest in Nyra, far too much interest. Each time his goblet emptied, he would call her over with a smirk, eyes tracking her every step like a predator sizing up prey. Every time she leaned forward to pour his wine, he would look at her as if she were something to be consumed. It made Corwin's stomach twist.

At first, he kept silent, watching with increasing discomfort, but when the knight brushed her hand "accidentally" for the third time, Corwin's jaw clenched so hard his teeth ached. Nyra did not deserve to be ogled like that. She did not deserve to be disrespected.

Darion, ever so observant, noticed the tension. His eyes flicked between Corwin and the young knight, a curious glint settling in his expression. He raised his glass and, with an overly dramatic gesture, tipped it sideways, spilling dark red wine across the pristine white tablecloth and the floor.

"Oh, clumsy me," Darion said with a smirk, feigning laughter, "Nyra, come clean this up at once." Without hesitation, Nyra stepped toward the spill, grabbing a cloth from the cart as she went. She moved with quiet obedience. But Corwin had seen it, he knew Darion. This was not clumsiness. This was a test. A power play.

Corwin reached out and gently caught Nyra's arm before she could kneel, "Nyra is *my* personal attendant," he said, his voice low and cutting, "she does not clean up *your* messes." There was a stillness in the room. The kind that came just before a storm. Nyra froze, caught between the two men, then slowly stepped back to Corwin's side, her face composed but her hands trembling just slightly at her sides.

Darion raised his brows, letting the act fall away. This was what he had wanted. A glimpse beneath Corwin's carefully guarded mask, "so what?" Darion sneered, "you have always allowed me to use your attendants. That is what they are here for, is it not?"

"Not anymore," Corwin replied, his tone sharp as steel, "from now on, you may *ask* the kitchen staff for assistance, or you will clean up after yourself."

Darion's mask cracked, anger flashing across his face like lightning. He stood, his chair scraping loudly against the stone floor, and in one swift movement, he grabbed Nyra by the shoulders and shoved her to the ground. Gasps echoed across the hall.

Corwin was on his feet before anyone else moved, fists slamming into the table with a thunderous crack, "that is *enough!*" he roared, his voice shaking the chandeliers, "where has your *respect* gone?!"

The guards by the entrance, finally shaken from their stillness, stepped forward with weapons drawn, surrounding the table with practiced speed. Darion looked around at the guards, the shocked noblemen, and finally at Corwin, whose expression was thunderous and unyielding. He had pushed too far.

Realizing the tide had turned, Darion scoffed bitterly, brushing off his robe as if the confrontation bored him. Without another word, he turned and strode from the dining hall, his boots echoing against the stone floor like distant drums of retreat. Silence settled like dust.

Then, the young knight, the one who had spent the evening watching Nyra like a hawk, staggered up from his seat. Still swaying from his drink, he stumbled over to her and extended a hand, "you alright, miss?" he slurred.

Nyra hesitated for half a breath before accepting his hand and rising to her feet. The crimson wine had soaked into the hem of her white dress, a vivid stain that bloomed like blood in fresh snow. Corwin stared at the spot, his jaw tight with anger he could no longer hide.

"You are all dismissed," he said coldly, eyes fixed on no one in particular.

"But, Your Majesty–" one of the noblemen started.

"Dismissed," Corwin snapped, sharper this time.

The room obeyed. Chairs scraped back, quiet mutters of discomfort floated through the air, and one by one, the noblemen exited the hall. The young knight lingered a moment longer than necessary, casting Nyra another too-friendly smile as he passed her. Corwin's glare followed him out the door. Then it was just the two of them.

"You mustn't let his actions affect you," Corwin said, approaching her slowly. "Darion is a selfish man who values power over everything else. His cruelty comes from weakness."

Nyra offered a soft, tired smile, "it is no worry," her eyes drifted down to the red stain on her dress, "I am sorry I ruined this… it was such a nice gown."

Corwin shook his head, disbelieving, "you were assaulted, and your first thought is to apologize for a stain you did not cause?"

Her smile faltered, and she looked down, "he was right, though. I *am* just a servant."

Corwin's heart twisted. Without thinking, he stepped forward and cupped her face in both hands, forcing her gaze back to his.

"No," he said, firm and desperate, "no one deserves to be treated that way, no matter their title."

His fingers softened against her cheeks, and for a moment, he simply looked at her. His expression, once rigid with royal discipline, melted into uncertainty. He realized too late how intimate the gesture had become. His hands dropped from her face with a quiet reluctance, and he stepped back quickly, clearing his throat as if to reclaim the crown that slipped each time he stood too close to her.

"You can help the kitchens tidy the mess," he said, his voice clipped again, "then report to my chambers before the end of the night." He did not wait for a reply. His boots echoed just like Darion's had, but his retreat was not cold, it was conflicted. A man walking away from the edge of something he did not yet understand, but could not deny.

Ten

You Will Find Your Peace Here

Nyra watched as the king disappeared down the corridor, his robe billowing behind him. She was touched by his concern but did not allow herself to dwell on it, there was still work to be done. When the kitchen staff entered to clear the table, she joined them without hesitation, her usual soft charm lighting her face. Even after all that had happened, she smiled at them all, hiding the weight that pressed against her chest.

A young woman, not much older than Nyra, entered the room, directing everyone with a voice that was firm yet kind. Though her orders were crisp and confident, she delivered them with a grace that softened the edges, punctuating her instructions with gentle manners.

When her eyes landed on Nyra, she crossed the room with purpose, "you must be Nyra,"

"Yes," Nyra replied, "and you are?"

"My name is Elowyn. I am the head chef here at Draymoor Castle," she said proudly, a faint glimmer of amusement in her eyes, "I hear you have been making quite the impression."

Nyra blinked, "so it seems. I am not sure why, though. I am just a servant."

Elowyn laughed, a light, genuine sound. "Oh, my dear, you are not just a servant. You are *the* servant. The king's personal attendant has always held a place of high honor in this castle. Some would even argue it is a more trusted position than the head of the guard."

Nyra's mouth parted slightly in shock, "you must be joking."

"I am not," Elowyn said with a knowing smile, "the former king held his attendant above even his most trusted knights. She eventually became queen."

Nyra's eyes widened, "Queen Lisanna was originally the king's attendant?"

Elowyn nodded, "she was. Not for very long, mind you. Many believed the king made her an attendant simply to bring her into the castle because he loved her." Nyra absorbed the new information slowly, feeling a heavy weight settle in her stomach. The enormity of her position loomed larger now, and with it, a gnawing doubt about her own worthiness crept in.

Elowyn must have seen the uncertainty in her eyes, because she touched Nyra's arm gently, "I am not saying you will end up queen," she said, smiling, "but perhaps it is time you started seeing more value in yourself."

Nyra's cheeks flushed at the suggestion, "if the personal attendant is so important, then why would King Corwin choose me?"

Elowyn's smile softened, touched with something almost like sympathy, "that is what everyone else is wondering, too. Personally," she added, lowering her voice, "I think he just wanted something different. King Corwin has always been a little astray from the usual paths."

"What makes you say that?" Nyra asked, curiosity lighting her voice.

Elowyn's smile turned nostalgic, "well, I worked under the previous king as a maid. Spent most of my days washing linens, tucked away where no one noticed. One afternoon, I went to the kitchen to collect towels for the laundry and found it empty. Being the foolish, spontaneous girl I was, I could not resist. I had always loved cooking, but I had never seen a kitchen so grand," her eyes shone a little as she spoke, the memory clearly still vivid.

"I lost myself in it, making my mother's bean soup, the only recipe I knew by heart. I did not think anyone would notice," Elowyn chuckled softly, "of course, I was caught. Locked away for a week, then thrown out by the king himself, ordered never to set foot in the palace again." Nyra's eyes widened, but Elowyn only laughed again, unbothered by the memory now.

"I always wondered if someone had tried my soup. Because not long after Corwin was crowned, he came and found me himself. Offered me the position of head chef without hesitation," her smile grew, "I have been as happy as I could ever dream to be since then. The king has a gift, you see, he finds real people. Not just the ones with the right names or lineage."

Nyra nodded slowly, absorbing every word. Between Elowyn and Seren, she was beginning to truly see the kind of king Corwin was. Not one who clung to the traditions of bloodlines and titles, but one who saw worth where others were blind. It struck her then, with quiet certainty that this was why the kingdom was growing stronger under Corwin's rule, because he dared to trust in hearts rather than crowns, in people rather than power.

"But if he were to follow in his father's footsteps and make you queen, I think you would fit the throne perfectly," Elowyn teased.

Nyra's face flushed hot, "oh, please, do not be ridiculous."

Elowyn laughed, unbothered, "you have to admit, though, he is a good-looking man."

Nyra turned away, hiding her smile as she placed the dishes into the sink. She began scrubbing them with exaggerated focus, "he does have some... decent features."

Elowyn bumped her shoulder playfully, "just *decent*?"

Nyra pushed her back, laughing under her breath, "if you are so fond of him, maybe *you* should become queen."

Elowyn threw her head back with a laugh and shook her head, flashing the gem on her finger, "I already have a king of my own."

Nyra smiled, her curiosity piqued, "you are married? How long?"

"A year now," Elowyn said warmly, "right around the time Corwin took the throne."

Nyra's smile deepened, "you got married and became the head chef all at once? That's quite the year."

Elowyn nodded, a proud gleam in her eyes, "it was a wonderful turn of events. I have no doubt **you will find your peace here**, too."

Nyra let out a soft sigh, the weight in her chest easing just a little, "I almost feel like I already have."

Elowyn's smile softened, "I am happy for you, and we are lucky to have you with us," she glanced over her shoulder, and pinched Nyra's cheek, "here, have some muffins. You look like you could use an extra snack."

Nyra laughed, shaking her head, "thank you, but I should really return to the king. I imagine he is expecting me."

"Well then, do not keep him waiting," Elowyn said with mock severity, before softening again, " but I will have some food sent to your room, just in case."

Nyra's heart warmed at her kindness, "you are too sweet. Thank you. Enjoy the rest of your evening."

"You as well, dear," Elowyn said, her smile lingering even after Nyra had gone.

Nyra excused herself to return to Corwin's chambers as instructed. She stepped out of the dining hall, the muffled sounds of the castle closing in around her. She paused for a moment just beyond the door, the tray of half-washed dishes and the warmth of Elowyn's laughter still lingering behind her.

For the first time in a long while, she realized she did not feel like an outsider. The castle, once so imposing and cold, felt almost like it was opening its arms to her, offering her a place, a purpose. And somewhere within those ancient stone walls, waiting beyond the winding corridors, was a king who had chosen *her* out of all the world. Nyra pressed a hand lightly against her chest, steadying the flutter there, and continued down the hall, her steps lighter than before.

Eleven

Dirty Dress

As she turned down the hallway, a figure emerged from the shadows, the young knight from earlier, weaving unsteadily on his feet, "hello again, miss," he slurred, his breath reeking with wine.

Nyra offered a polite smile, attempting to sidestep him, "good evening, sir."

"Do not give me that 'sir' nonsense," he said, reaching for her waist, "call me Ronan."

She tensed beneath his hand but kept her composure, "are you lost? I would be happy to show you to the guest chambers. They are near the king's quarters, so I can lead the way."

Ronan grinned, staggering as he tried to follow her, "what a sweet thing you are," he mumbled, "please, show me to my chambers."

They reached the stairwell, but Ronan stumbled after just a few steps and nearly fell backward. Nyra instinctively caught him, slipping his arm over her shoulders to help him climb. His weight pressed into her, his words dissolving into nonsense murmured too close to her ear. At the top of the stairs, she gently pulled away, but he continued to reach for her. She ignored it and guided him down the hall to his room.

"Ah yes, this one is mine," he said, fumbling with the handle before opening the door. He stepped inside, then turned to her, "come in for a moment, miss. I need your help with something."

"I am sorry," Nyra said firmly, "I must return to the king."

"Oh, come on. Just one moment," he said.

"No, I must–" but before she could finish without warning, he grabbed her arm and yanked her inside. She stumbled over his grasp, catching herself just as he slammed the door shut behind her.

"Ronan..." her voice shook, "I need to go. Please move."

"No, no. The king does not own you. He can not keep you all to himself," he sneered, advancing on her. Nyra backed away, hands raised to create distance, but her heels met the edge of the bed. Ronan grinned, enjoying the trap he had made.

"Ronan, please," she whispered, "let me leave."

"Not yet," he said darkly. He grabbed her waist again, drawing her close.

"The king's orders–" she tried to speak, but he clamped a hand over her mouth.

"I do not want to hear another word about that pathetic king. You are mine now," he growled. He threw her onto the bed, and Nyra's breath caught in her throat. Her heart pounded in her chest as Ronan loomed over her, crawling onto the mattress.

"What a **dirty dress** you have on," Ronan smiled, "how about you take it off?" His hand found the hem of her dress and began to lift it, his grip rough and greedy.

Through her panic, Nyra's mother's voice echoed in her mind: *"do not ever let a man lay his hands on you, do you understand? I do not care if he is a peasant or the king himself, you hit him with everything you have, Nyra."*

Without hesitation, Nyra's hand shot to the bedside table. Her fingers curled around a heavy brass candle holder. With every ounce of strength she had, she swung it. The metal collided with Ronan's skull with a sickening crack. He groaned and faltered, giving her just enough time to wriggle out from under him. She bolted for the door.

His hand snagged the fabric of her sleeve, tearing it as she pulled away. Nyra did not stop. She ran breathless and heart racing through the corridors to Corwin's chamber. Without knocking, she burst through the door, slamming it shut behind her, her chest heaving as she braced herself against it.

Corwin's head snapped toward the door as it burst open, startled by the sudden intrusion. His breath caught when he saw Nyra. Her chest heaving, eyes wide with panic, a torn dress clinging to her trembling frame. He was on his feet in an instant, crossing the room in a few long strides.

"What happened?" he asked urgently, already reaching for her.

"R-Ronan," she stammered, struggling for breath, "he was drunk and lost... I tried to help him..."

Corwin took her shaking hands in his, steadying them gently, "breathe. You are safe now. Just breathe. Tell me what happened, Nyra."

She closed her eyes, forcing air into her lungs as she tried to gather herself, "I offered to show him to his room. I was heading this way anyway. But then... he pulled me inside. He shut the door behind me and would not let me leave. He– he pushed me onto his bed, and I panicked. I did not know what to do, he would not listen– so I..." Nyra's voice caught. She raised a hand to her mouth, eyes filling with fear. She realized what she was about to admit and to whom. Assaulting a knight could mean death, regardless of the circumstances.

Corwin's expression hardened, his jaw tightening, "tell me," he said, low and firm.

"I struck him," she whispered, "with a brass candle holder on the side of the head," she looked down, shame coloring her voice, "I am sorry... I just– I could not let him..."

Corwin's eyes widened slightly. He took a step back, processing her words, "you understand what the punishment for harming a knight is, do you?"

Nyra nodded quickly, tears welling in her eyes, "yes, I know. But please... you have to believe me. He would not stop. I swear I did not mean to."

"I believe you," Corwin interrupted, his voice soft but strained, "I believe every word, but..." he ran a hand through his hair, turning away for a moment as the weight of his position settled on his shoulders, "this is... complicated. You harmed a knight, even in defense. If word gets out, if the court finds out, they will demand your punishment. They will say the law must be upheld."

Nyra's voice was barely audible, "so... what happens now?"

Corwin turned back to her. There was a storm in his eyes of fury, guilt, protectiveness, and something dangerous for a king to feel, "I will handle it," he said, "you will say nothing. I will deal with Ronan myself."

"But–"

"Nyra," Corwin stepped closer, lowering his voice to a near whisper, "I will not let them touch you. Do you understand me? You did what you had to do. You fought back. You survived. Just like you always have."

Nyra nodded, her head bowed, "thank you... You are too kind to me," she sniffled.

"Nonsense," Corwin said firmly, "you deserve every bit of kindness given to you."

"You are–" she began, but the door burst open before she could finish. A guard stormed inside and seized her roughly, yanking her away from Corwin.

"Forgive me, Your Majesty," the guard said, already clamping cold iron shackles around her wrists, "but we have received word that Nyra has assaulted Sir Ronan. Prince Darion has ordered her taken to the cellar immediately."

Corwin's rage ignited, "release her at once! You follow my commands, not Darion's!"

As if summoned by the accusation, Darion entered the room, followed closely by Ronan, his head now wrapped in bandages, and a few others. Darion wore a triumphant smile.

"Oh brother," Darion began smoothly, "I must apologize. You spoke so highly of your charming attendant, but her touch is not nearly as gentle as her gaze. As you can see," he gestured to Ronan's head, "she is not as innocent as she appears."

Corwin's eyes blazed, "I have reason to believe she was defending herself."

"Defending herself?" Ronan scoffed, "is that what she told you? The truth is, she came onto me, throwing herself at me, demanding intimacy. I refused, and she lost her temper."

Corwin's expression darkened in disgust, "your story does not hold weight, Ronan. You stared at her like a starving dog all through dinner."

Ronan scowled, "I may have looked, Your Majesty, but I have standards. I would not waste myself with a *servant*."

Corwin stepped forward, fury tightening every line of his face, "enough. I have dealt with enough of your kind to know a lie when I hear it. Nyra speaks with honesty and grace."

Darion raised an eyebrow and stepped closer, "with all due respect, Your Majesty, you have known this girl for less than a day. Can you truly vouch for her character?"

Corwin moved to close the distance between them, but to his shock, the guard raised a hand and stepped in his way, blocking him. Corwin froze, stunned by the defiance. The power in the room shifted like a tide turning against him.

Darion stood tall behind the guard, a smug smile stretching across his lips, "she is just a servant, Corwin. What value does she really have?"

Corwin's fist flew without hesitation, striking Darion clean across the face, "more valuable than the lying rat you have brought into my halls."

Darion staggered back, holding his cheek, stunned, "you would strike me for her? A servant? Have you lost your mind?!" his expression morphed into something more calculating, "you are not acting like yourself. At dinner, you were protective. Possessive. It is almost as if... someone is influencing you."

Ronan's voice chimed in, venomous and smug, "I have heard stories from the villages on the outer wall. They grow a plant that induces trance-like states... hypnosis. Coincidence, Your Majesty, that your first encounter with her involved fruit?"

The guard added, "come to think of it, yes. She offered him an apple, did she not?"

Corwin scoffed in disbelief, "you can not be serious. You think I am under some kind of spell?" They all exchanged glances, some uncertain, others already convinced.

"It would explain your behavior," Darion said coldly.

"This is lunacy!" Corwin shouted, "release her and leave my chambers at once!" But it was already too late. Darion gave the guard a silent nod. Before Corwin could react, the guards turned on him. One seized his arms from behind, restraining him as he thrashed to break free.

"I am sorry, brother," Darion said solemnly, "we will not let her control you any longer. You will thank us... eventually."

Twelve

I Am Yours

The guards dragged Corwin and Nyra down the winding stairwell, their boots echoing like war drums in the cold stone corridor. The air grew damp and stale as they descended into the basement, the torches on the walls flickering dimly against moss-covered stone. Darion followed behind with smug precision, grabbing the keys from Corwin's belt without hesitation. He strode to the heavy iron door of the cellar and unlocked it with a rusty clank.

"Throw them in," he ordered.

The guards obeyed. Nyra was flung across the small stone cell like a ragdoll, her back slamming into the cold wall. She cried out softly at the impact. The keys jingled mockingly in Darion's hand as he locked the cells behind them with a final, echoing *click*.

"Darion, you son of a bitch!" Corwin's voice thundered through the cellar. He lunged at the bars, rattling them with fury, "open this door right now!"

Darion strolled over, standing just beyond the reach of Corwin's outstretched arms, his face the picture of false sympathy, "I will, my dear brother... as soon as the hypnosis wears off," he glanced at Nyra with a cold smirk, "and she is dead. Until then, I can not trust a word you say."

Corwin spat through the bars, hitting Darion square in the face, "you are not my brother."

Darion wiped his cheek slowly, not breaking eye contact, "the real Corwin would never say that," he said with mock sadness, "you always loved playing the hero, right?"

Corwin's eyes burned, "only because you were so desperate to play the villain."

Darion chuckled, stepping back, "well, we all have our roles to play," he gave one last glance over his shoulder, "sleep tight, Your Majesty."

"Get back here, Darion!" Corwin roared, slamming his fists against the bars, "I *am* the king! You are bound by oath to obey me!"

But it was no use. Darion and the guards climbed the steps without a word, and a moment later, the heavy door slammed shut, sealing them in silence. Corwin exhaled sharply, resting his forehead against the cold iron. He clenched the bars in defeat, his breath shallow and fast. Then he heard soft sobbing.

He turned and saw her, in the cell next to his, curled tightly in the corner. Nyra was huddled on the ground, her arms wrapped around her knees, her face buried in her arms. Her shoulders trembled with each quiet, broken sob. Corwin's heart sank.

"Come here," Corwin held out his hand through the bars that separated them. The cold iron stood like a cruel reminder of everything that was lost, but his voice, low, steady, and laced with longing cut through the space like warmth in winter.

Nyra looked up, wiping the tears from her eyes with the frayed sleeve of her dress. Her body trembled as she stood up, as if each movement was made through the weight of grief. The stones beneath her bare feet were damp as she stepped forward. Her hand shook as she placed it in his.

Corwin pulled her in gently, as close as the bars would allow. His touch was gentle as if he feared even now he might break her further.

Slowly, he lifted her hand to his lips and pressed a kiss to its back. His touch was soft and aching with all the words he could not say.

Her eyes welled again, this time from something deeper than sorrow, "I am not deserving of your kindness," she whispered, voice nearly lost in the silence.

Corwin shook his head, his eyes never leaving hers, "you are worthy of so much more than a kiss on the hand."

A tired smile ghosted across her face, "you are a great king," she said softly, "and the best man I have ever met."

His jaw clenched, "you are foolish if you think I am a great man."

"Then dress me in a jester's attire," she replied, a fragile defiance in her voice, "because if a man of your status can look down to someone as meaningless as me and still show love, then you are far better than any ruler this land has seen."

His hands tightened slightly around hers, "you are not meaningless."

The silence between them stretched, full of unspoken things, promises that could never be fulfilled, futures that would never come to pass, and a love that bloomed in the wrong place. And still, in that dim and crumbling cell, surrounded by stone and shadows, they held onto each other like the world was crumbling around them, because in many ways, it already had.

"You are right, I am not meaningless, because I am not going to die as nobody and be left to be forgotten. I get to die in sacrifice to my king," her voice was steady. She met his eyes with a quiet smile, the kind that had not made peace with fate but still clung to the hope of being remembered.

Corwin brushed his fingers across Nyra's cheek, gentle as falling snow. He wiped away the traces of her sorrow, though it felt like trying to stop the tide with his bare hands. His gaze held no royal pride, only a raw, aching humility, "I will get you out of this. I will not let anyone hurt you."

For a moment, she allowed herself the comfort of his touch, leaning into it like a flower toward the sun. Her eyes fluttered closed, "I will be killed whether or not you side with me," she whispered, "their minds are set. They believe I am some sort of witch who has you under a spell. They will not listen to you... not until I am dead."

The words struck him like arrows, each syllable cutting itself deep in his chest, "it will not happen," he said, his voice low, "I am the king. They have to obey me," but even as he spoke, doubt lingered in his eyes, like a man standing in the middle of a crumbling bridge, shouting at the wind to save him.

Nyra sighed and looked at him with a tenderness that seemed to age her by years, "you remind me of my mother," she said, "stubborn and selfish. But not selfish in the way that you only care about yourself... selfish in the way that you only care about things that are important to you. It is what makes a protector."

Corwin smiled softly, brushing a stray lock of hair from her face with the backs of his fingers, "are you going to spend all this time in the cell trying to flatter me?" There was a faint teasing in his voice, but it was small, like a sheet trying to hide the sorrow underneath.

"I am just telling you the truth," she said, her eyes shimmering, "my family died long ago. I have been alone for years, giving up pieces of myself just to survive. No one ever listened when I cried. No one ever cared," she took a shaky breath, her voice catching, "but here... I wore the finest clothes I have ever touched. I ate the largest meal I have ever seen. I got to play the piano again and feel music in my fingers after so long. And someone listened. Someone saw me," her voice cracked, "even if it was only for a day... It was the best day of my life." She paused, her eyes swimming with tears, "I am sorry I failed you as a servant," she said, "but I will forever be in your debt for giving me this... this taste of life."

Corwin's smile faded. His chest tightened, the sting of her words cutting deeper than any blade, "why are you talking to me like you are giving up?"

Her lips trembled, "I am not giving up," she whispered, "I am saying goodbye," and with that, the tears came again, pouring down her cheeks like rain on a dying flame.

Cowrin's heart cracked at the sight. That brave, resilient spark that had always lived behind her eyes now flickered so faintly it was almost gone, "do not say goodbye," he murmured, his voice thick with emotion, "you are not going anywhere." Nyra did not respond right away. She only looked at him, studying every line of his face like she was trying to memorize it. Her fingers tightened gently around his.

"I am scared," she finally whispered, "not of dying, but of disappearing, of being forgotten, of the world continuing on like I never existed."

"You will not be forgotten," Corwin said, firmly. "Not by me. I will remember everything. Your laugh, the way you played the piano, how you looked at me like I was just a man and not a crown."

Nyra gave a soft, watery smile, "that is all I ever saw. A man who looked tired of being worshipped."

"And you," Corwin murmured, "you were the only one who ever looked at me like I was worth more than the throne I sit on." He reached through the bars again, brushing the side of her hand with his thumb, "you were a stranger in a village, and I did not know your name, and still, I think... I think I loved you the moment you handed me that apple."

Nyra let out a soft, broken laugh, "you are hopeless."

"**I am yours**," he said without hesitation.

She grew quiet at that. The silence between them was no longer filled with dread, It felt almost peaceful, like a gentle current after a storm. The stone walls around them did not seem as suffocating anymore, not when they were both awake in the dark, holding onto each other.

Nyra slid down to the floor of her cell, her legs too weak to stand any longer, "will you stay with me? Even if it is just through these bars?"

"I am not going anywhere," he promised, already lowering himself to the ground opposite her. He stretched his hand through the narrow space between their cells until their fingers found each other again. The floor was cold, the air damp, but somehow their linked hands made it bearable. Nyra curled up beside the bars, her cheek resting against the stone, her other hand clutching Corwin's like it was a lifeline. He mirrored her on the other side, his gaze fixed on her face.

"I wish I could have taken you riding," he said softly, "to show you the cliffs at daybreak, when the mist rises from the hills and the world looks like it is holding its breath."

Nyra smiled faintly, "and I would have wanted to hear you sing. You have a voice, I can tell. One of those low ones that barely rises above a whisper, but it makes everything stop to listen."

He huffed a small laugh, "I do not sing."

"Not yet," she murmured, her voice growing sleepier, "but if you ever do... sing for me."

"I will."

Their hands squeezed gently, as if anchoring each other to this fragile moment. Their eyes stayed open just a little longer, reluctant to lose even a second of it.

"I feel safe with you," she breathed.

"I have never felt safer with anyone," he replied, his voice thick with emotion.

Silence settled again, heavier this time, not from sorrow but from exhaustion. Their breathing slowed together, soft and steady, matching in rhythm. Neither knew when sleep overtook them, only that they were holding hands through iron bars, hearts barely inches apart, and dreaming, for the first time in what felt like forever, of something beautiful.

Thirteen

Thank You For Everything

The sound of footsteps echoing down the stairwell woke them up, like the ticking of a clock counting down the final seconds. Both of their hearts pounded, sensing that the moment they feared had arrived.

From the shadows emerged Darion, his face twisted with the authority he always craved, followed by the guards, "your pit is ready, servant," he sneered, his words dripping with disgust.

"Do not touch her!" Corwin's voice rang out, fierce and commanding. But it was hollow now, stripped of all his power.

One of the guards stepped forward, grabbing the keys from his belt. The jingle of metal felt like a death bell. The cell door creaked open, and rough hands seized Nyra, yanking her away without hesitation. She cried out, struggling, but it was no use. Corwin reached forward through the bars. He caught her hand, both of them locking eyes as he held on with everything he had, their fingers entwined in a desperate knot. The guards pulled harder. He pulled back harder still. It became a brutal game of tug of war with her life as the prize.

Darion said nothing. He only turned his cold gaze to the other guards and gave a single nod. Chains clinked. Nyra's breath froze as she watched them approach Corwin's cell with iron shackles. Her heart dropped. She knew what they were about to do. Not to her, but to him.

The king turned, eyes flickering over to the approaching guards, realization dawning slow and heavy. His hold on her tightened like a man trying to anchor himself against the tide. Panic crept into his eyes, not for himself, but for her. For what it would mean when they tore him away. But it was too late. She saw it before he did. The way the guards circled him, the way their hands reached for steel and chain. She knew what came next.

Nyra looked at him one last time, memorizing the shape of his face in the low torchlight: the flecks of gold in his eyes, the crease between his brows, the way his mouth trembled as he refused to let go. And for a moment, the world fell silent. No footsteps. No shouting. No rattling iron or cruel commands. Just the sound of two hearts beating at once.

"**Thank you for everything**," she whispered, her voice barely a breath, but loud enough for him to hear. Loud enough to break him.

And then... She let go.

Her fingers slipped from his, slowly, like petals falling from a dying flower. Her hand dropped to her side, and in that instant, it felt as though all the air had been sucked from the room. Corwin's arm hung through the bars, still reaching, still hoping, still not understanding how she could have released him when he was holding on for dear life.

"Nyra...?" His voice cracked as her name left his mouth, a sound filled with disbelief and betrayal and aching sorrow all at once. The guards yanked her away, but she did not fight them this time. Then the guards were gone with her.

Corwin, once a king, once a god in his kingdom, fell to his knees in helplessness. The air in the dungeon turned cold. He stayed like that, hand still reaching, breathing hard, heart thundering in the space she had just stood grasping for a ghost now.

Darion watched with an unreadable expression, but somewhere deep in his gaze was a glint of satisfaction, like a puppeteer who had just clipped the final thread before following them up the stairs. Corwin did not scream. He did not rage. He simply dropped his head against the bars, looking down at his hand like it had just been severed from his soul. His eyes closed and whispered her name again like a prayer he knew would never be answered.

"Nyra..."

The heavy door at the top of the stairwell slammed shut with finality, casting the cellar in suffocating silence. Darkness swallowed him whole, leaving behind nothing but a man, a promise he could not keep, and the echoes of a goodbye that shattered everything.

A sudden commotion outside interrupted the heavy silence. Corwin's head turned toward the sound. He stood on the bed in the cell and pressed his face to the small, barred window. What he saw made his blood run cold. The courtyard had been transformed into a scene of execution. In its center was the pit, and now the flames of hatred and fear were ready to be fed. They dragged her out like a carcass, her limbs dangling, lifeless. She did not resist. She did not scream. Her head hung to the side as though her soul had already left. Corwin felt his heart stop. Her body was limp, a puppet with its strings cut as they hoisted her onto the wooden stake, arms stretched out in a horrid crucifixion. She had surrendered, and it killed him more than anything.

"This girl has been living among us as a traitor," Darion declared, his voice booming with pride, "she has bewitched the King into her submission, and now she will pay for her crimes." He stood before her as though reveling in a coronation rather than an execution, chest puffed and eyes alight with triumph. The courtyard, filled with nobles and commoners, a rippling murmur of judgment. It slithered through the air like smoke, curling into every ear, every doubt, suspicion.

They did not see her, not truly. Not the girl who once marveled at sunlight breaking through stained glass. Not the girl who touched piano keys as if they were pieces of her own soul. No. To them, she was nothing now but the villain in someone else's tale. A witch, a snake, a seductive shadow dragging down the crown. Corwin could do nothing.

He stood cloaked in shadow behind the bars of the prison, his arms threaded through the iron as if he might tear the whole thing down with sheer will alone. His fingers clenched so tightly they trembled, the bones beneath his skin bulging, his knuckles pale as snow.

He should have spoken. Fought. Died in her place. But he hesitated. He had let them take her. Had let them silence him.

If only I had kept my heart hidden.

The thought hit him like a hammer. If only he had been stronger, colder, what a king was meant to be. If only he had looked at her and seen nothing but a servant. If only he had not invited her in, not given her warmth, not let her bloom in the garden of his affection. If only he had protected her by never loving her at all.

His breath caught, ragged and sharp. The torch's light flickered across her face as the guard approached. Her expression was calm. Too calm. Like she had already made peace with the fire to come. Like she knew this was the end. Still she did not look for rescue. She looked up to the sky. The crowd leaned in. Corwin shrank back.

This is my fault.

Every heartbeat pounded with the weight of that truth.

This is my fault.

Every breath scorched his lungs like he was the one about to burn. He had worn a crown forged in centuries of legacy and blood, but it had never felt heavier than it did now, watching the only person who had ever seen him as more than a monarch dragged to the altar of public sacrifice.

I gave her the castle... and led her straight to the gallows.

He had promised to protect her. Sworn it, with every fiber of who he was. Yet now, he stood behind iron, gagged by his own shame, forced to watch the world destroy the woman who had made him feel human. The torch was raised. The flame danced, hungry and bright. Corwin sank to his knees behind the bars, unable to scream, unable to sob. Only the guilt remained sharp and endless, coiling tighter around his throat than any chain.

The chains chafed against Nyra wrists where they held her fast, binding her arms above her head. Every breath was an effort, tight, shallow, drawn through a throat dry with dust and fear. The wooden platform beneath her bare feet felt foreign, like the stage of a play she had never agreed to perform in. The crowd stretched out before her, a sea of faces turned upward, not with empathy, but anticipation. Darion's voice rang out like a drumbeat of death.

Nyra did not flinch at the words. Not anymore. At first, they stung. Those falsehoods, the venom poured into her name. Witch. Seductress. Spy. She slowly looked up waiting for someone, *anyone*, to speak in her defense. But that hope had withered fast, and now her heart sat hollow beneath her ribs, like a candle burned to its end. She stared out into the crowd. They did not see her. To them, she was a symbol of corruption. A danger to the throne. A lesson. She could feel their eyes like knives. Some looked on with disgust. Others with thrill. But none with compassion.

Her eyes drifted upward. Above the courtyard, the clouds hung low and heavy, as if the heavens themselves were mourning. A breeze stirred her hair, brushing it across her face like a farewell touch. She closed her eyes and breathed it in. One last breath.

Darion was still speaking. She heard him, vaguely, like a distant echo carried on wind and fire, "she has turned my brother against us. Twisted his mind, taken advantage of his grace. But justice will not bend to treachery. Today, we remind the people: no one is above the law. Not even the king's whore," the word struck her like a lash.

She knew Corwin was somewhere in the tower, watching. She could almost feel him, like a tether through the sky, stretched between her and the stone bars where he was being held. Her heart ached at the thought of him, the way he had looked at her with such helpless pain. She hated that he had to watch this. But more than that, she hated that he would blame himself.

"Do not blame yourself, Corwin," she thought, *"please do not."*

Because she did not regret this. The piano. The laughter in the garden. The way his hand had held hers like it was the only thing in the world worth saving. If she had the choice to do it all again, even knowing where it ended, she would.

She breathed in, the chains biting deeper into her skin. Still, she stood. Still, she did not break. As Darion's voice echoed over the square, painting her as a monster, Nyra let her eyes flutter closed once more, not in surrender, but in memory. *His touch. His voice. His promise.* In her last moments, she would remember that. Not the crowd. Not the crucifix. Not Darion. *Him.*

Fourteen

Forbidden Snow

"Take this as a warning to anyone who tries to cross the king!" Darion shouted, raising a clenched fist. A cruel irony. He gestured to the guard who dropped the torch into the pit. The dry straw caught instantly. Fire roared to life at the base of the wood, crawling upward with hunger. The flames licked the bottom of her feet, at first like teasing fingers, hot and sharp. Then came the bite. Real fire. Real pain.

Nyra's body jerked violently against the chains, all thought shattered by the searing agony. Instinct clawed through her chest, overriding every whisper of surrender she had tried to cradle in her heart. Her heels twisted midair, searching for escape where there was none. The chains held fast, cutting deeper into her skin with each jerk, but it was the fire that consumed her.

A scream tore from her throat. A raw, primal, a sound not made of words but of something ancient and soul-deep. It pierced the air, climbing up to the sky like a plea to gods who had stopped listening long ago. It bounced off stone walls, slipped between the cracks in marble, and wormed its way into the bone of everyone watching.

The fire climbed higher, a cruel, greedy beast. It devoured the hem of her dress first, that still carried the wine stain. Then it rose, swallowing the fabric in orange waves. Her skin blistered. Smoke curled around her like the fingers of death, filling her lungs with heat and ash. The metal chains burned up quickly, pressing against her body as the iron links welded to her skin.

The scent of burning hair, of flesh, of something sacred being undone filled the courtyard. The stench burned just as much as the flame. Violently bitter and sharp, poisoning the air with chemical sweetness that clung to the skin of everyone around. Her features were slowly disappearing, melting away the girl as delicate as snow. Nyra's head fell back, her scream fractured into hoarse sobs. Tears carved trails down her soot-covered cheeks, vanishing into the smoke as quickly as they fell. Her eyes searched the sky above.

The fire danced around her legs, curling like a devil's claw, pulling her closer to oblivion. Her body trembled violently, not in fear, but in unbearable pain. The heat was no longer just outside her, it was inside her, crawling beneath her skin, consuming her from the core outward. Her nerves sparked like lightning, her heart a frantic drumbeat in a closing cage.

Somewhere in the crowd, a child began to cry. Somewhere, a man turned away. But Corwin did not turn away, and Nyra, through the smoke, through the fire, opened her eyes one last time, searching. Not for mercy or salvation. Just for *him*.

Her cries turned to sobs, to gasps, and then... to silence. The fire went on much longer than her soul left, and yet, he still watched. Corwin could not look away. His love burned before him. All he could do was mourn her in silence, while her execution was praised as a lesson under his own name.

It all happened too fast. Too loud, too bright, too final. And now... it was just *still*. The screams had vanished, swallowed by the fire, and the silence that remained was somehow louder, like a hand wrapped around the throat of the world. The air was thick with smoke and ash, but even thicker with the weight of what had just occurred. It pressed against Corwin's chest, like grief trying to take the shape of something physical.

He did not remember moving. Did not remember crossing the stone floor or gripping the edge of the narrow window like it was the only thing tethering him to reality. But there he stood, still dressed in the robes of a king, yet feeling more like a ghost, staring out at the courtyard below. His eyes locked on the charred remains of the woman he loved. Or at least, what was left of her.

Her body hung from the blackened pole, the chains still tight around her wrists, her limbs slack and unmoving, scorched beyond recognition. Her skin, once kissed by moonlight and soft as silk, was now blackened, cracked, and ruined. Smoke curled upward from the dying embers beneath her feet, carrying with it the last pieces of her, ribbons of ash dancing on the wind, as if the world itself could not bear to let her go quietly.

The pole stood like a monument. She had once filled that space with song, with laughter, with courage that burned brighter than any flame. And now she was reduced to nothing more than a silhouette of suffering. A punishment for loving him.

Corwin's mouth was dry. His throat ached, but no sound came out. He wanted to scream, to shatter the window, to fall to his knees and weep until the earth opened and swallowed him whole, but all he could do was stare. His mind grasped at fragments, but they dissolved as quickly as they came.

The way she used to look at him like he was more than a crown. The way her fingers danced over piano keys like they were breathing. The way she had smiled, even when terrified. Even when in pain. Even when dying.

Corwin leaned forward, his forehead pressing against the cold stone of the window ledge. His eyes burned, not from smoke, but from the tears he had held back for too long. He had failed her. Not just as a king, but as a man. As the one who had promised to protect her, who had told her he would get her out of this, who had whispered comforts into her hands through iron bars and then stood helpless as they dragged her away. He had not fought hard enough. Had not broken free. Had not saved her. And now, all that remained of Nyra was ash and silence.

The crowd began to disperse. Silent heads bowed. They did not speak. They did not cry. They just walked away, shielding their eyes from the aftermath as if they had not just watched a soul burn. Darion turned on his heel, the corners of his mouth curled upward in twisted satisfaction. He walked off with a self-satisfied stride, victorious in the eyes of no one but himself. Corwin remained motionless. More guards arrived to clean the scene, their movements mechanical, unaffected. They carried water, tools, and ropes. To them, it was another task, another body, another pit.

The wind blew gently. It brushed past the charred pyre, lifting a fine wisp of ash into the air. The ash drifted like feathers, carried across the courtyard and through the narrow slits of the King's cell window falling on him like **_forbidden snow_**. It touched his face, delicate and warm. The ash settled on his lips as if the remains of Nyra were giving him the kiss he never got to have.

"Thank you for everything."

PART TWO

Fifteen

Goodbye Brother

The world was quiet. Corwin's mind was a haze. Darion descended down the stairs. The same metal-clinking footsteps as the first time. The guard beside him opened the cell door.

"Forgive me, Corwin, for having to treat you so vulgarly," Darion said, "I did it for your own safety." He reeked of smoke. Corwin turned his head slowly from the window, eyes landing on the man whose hands carried Nyra's blood. Darion, a man he once considered family, stood before him now as a monster.

Ash clung to Corwin's robes like a tether, as if Nyra's spirit refused to leave him. When he looked at Darion, all he could see was her blackened, broken body. The girl he loved. The fire. The screams that wrenched from her throat. Corwin let go of his mind and let his heart take over. And his heart wanted only one thing.

Justice.

His eyes flicked to the guard's belt, to the sword. Without hesitation, he seized it. It had been a year since Corwin had held a weapon. Since he became king, he had not been a warrior fighting for the people, only a voice buried behind closed doors. But the weight of the sword in his grip brought it all back. The memory came fast.

"Faster, Corwin! You are getting sloppy!" the king barked. Corwin narrowed his eyes, jaw tightening. Across from him, the knight raised his wooden

blade. Corwin swung. Again. Again. But no matter how much force he put into it, he could not land a single blow. Frustration surged.

He threw his sword to the ground. "I am focused! I just... I will never be as strong as you!"

His father chuckled and stepped forward, laying a hand on his shoulder, "you know," he said, "I said the same thing to my father."

Corwin blinked, "you did?"

"I did," the king nodded, "I struggled too, but do you know what he told me?"

Corwin shook his head.

"He said: Strength does not come from the body, it comes from the heart. If you want to defeat your enemy, you must lead with your heart." Corwin remembered the lesson and the weight of it. He had picked up his sword again. And when he faced the knight once more, he did not fight for pride or approval, he fought like the boy who had lost his mother. With focus. With fury. With purpose. Strike after strike until he gained the upper hand until the knight fell, disarmed, at his feet. He stood over him in triumph as his father praised him.

But this was not the training yard. This was the cellar. The guard below him was not holding a wooden blade. He was dead, a real sword buried in his chest. The man that used to serve him with undying loyalty, lay on the ground with blank eyes. Like a sock without a foot, nothing but an empty shell. Corwin's chest heaved. Blood soaked into the ash on his robes. He looked up. Darion stood frozen, pale, eyes wide. He had always known Corwin was strong, but this? This was something else. Corwin's balance of mind and body, his precise calm beneath the rage... it was *terrifying*. Darion stumbled backward. Then he turned and ran for the stairs

Corwin watched him run faster than he ever had before. Fear surged through Darion's limbs, lending him strength, speed, desperation. But it was not enough. It had never been enough. Not against Corwin. That's what had always separated them, even as children. That is why Corwin wore the crown. Because he was stronger, faster, and smarter.

He caught Darion by the shoulders and slammed him to the ground the same way Darion had thrown Nyra. He scrambled across the floor, hands slipping on the stone, trying to claw his way out of reach. Corwin stalked forward, slow and sure, like a hunter closing in on wounded prey.

"Please, Corwin!" Darion gasped, eyes wide with panic, "I thought you were bewitched. I was only doing what Father would have done!"

Corwin's gaze burned, "do not lie to me!" he kicked Darion hard in the side, sending him reeling, "you never cared about me, you only ever cared about the throne."

Darion flinched, pressing himself back against the cold wall, "brother, listen to me–"

"Shut up!" Corwin's voice cracked, thick with fury and betrayal, "I loved you. I trusted you. My whole life. But these last few years... I do not know who you are anymore. You are not my brother. You are a monster."

Darion's face twisted in grief, rage, envy all at once, "the crown should have been mine!" he shouted, "I was the one who listened to Father like his words were words of the gods. You were just a reckless, arrogant child. And still... he loved *you* more than anything."

Corwin's grip on the sword tightened, "so this is about jealousy? That is your excuse for murder?"

Darion's voice broke, "I just wanted them to look at me the way they looked at you. I wanted Mother and Father to love me like they loved you. I did not want to be forgotten. I did not want to live in your shadow. I just wanted to matter."

"You did matter," Corwin said softly, his voice raw, "you mattered to *me*." His breath trembled with emotion as he looked down at the boy he once protected, once admired, once loved more than anything. He searched Darion's eyes, hoping, *begging*, for a trace of that brother to still be there.

But Darion only laughed, bitter and cold, "you know what happens to the people you love, Corwin. They die. Just like that servant girl I burned on the pole," his smile curled cruelly, "you are pathetic, you always have been. You are not fit to be king."

Corwin's body stilled. He raised his sword, grief and rage crashing in waves beneath his skin. He looked into Darion's face one last time–

The stars were just starting to peek through the twilight when the two boys tumbled into the grass outside the castle gates, laughing like they had just conquered a kingdom. Corwin was twelve. Darion, eight.

"You cheated!" Darion shouted through a giggle, rolling onto his back.

"I won," Corwin said smugly, panting, "that is different."

"You stepped out of the ring."

"There is no ring," Corwin said, flopping beside him, "we are in the middle of a field."

Darion huffed, "still counts as cheating." Corwin turned his head to look at him. His brother's golden hair was sticking to his forehead with sweat, and there was a smudge of dirt across one cheek. He looked ridiculous.

"You will be strong like me one day," Corwin said.

Darion stared up at the stars, voice softer now, "father says I am too small to be anything."

Corwin frowned, "Father says lots of things, that does not mean he is right." There was a silence between them, filled only by the chirp of crickets and the rustle of wind through tall grass.

Then Corwin sat up and poked Darion's side, "wanna know something?"

"What?"

"You are my favorite person in the whole kingdom."

Darion grinned with his crooked teeth, "even more than the horse master who sneaks you biscuits?"

Corwin paused, "okay, second favorite." They both burst into laughter.

"Goodbye brother," were the last words Darion heard before he was pierced through the heart.

"You are my second favorite too."

"Who is the first?"

"The baker who makes the biscuits."

Sixteen

The Garden

Corwin ran up the stairwell, dizzy and disoriented. Between Nyra's death and the blood still drying on his hands, he could barely feel his own heartbeat. He shoved past guards without a word, stumbling through the castle until the stone opened up to the sky. The courtyard. He reached it just as they began to lower her body from the pole.

"Stop!" Corwin shouted. His voice cracked like a whip across the square. People turned, guards, servants, nobles, eyes wide as they saw their king, breathless and pale, moving like a man on the edge of breaking.

The guards hesitated, but one look at his wild, desperate, unflinching face and they stepped aside. The air reeked of burnt flesh. The smell clung to skin and throat, thick and bitter. It turned his stomach and stung his eyes.

Corwin knelt as they released the chains, catching her remains in his arms as gently as if she were still whole. A girl once radiant with life with lush hair, fair skin, eyes like light on winter snow now lay in his embrace as a blackened husk. Her body was nearly gone. Bone wrapped in charcoal flesh. Fingers fused. Skin hardened into a leathery shell. He held her like she was still there, still Nyra. A wave of nausea and grief struck him.

He tried to lift her, but parts of her body crumbled in his hands, falling to dust between his fingers. His breath caught. He wrapped her in his cloak, an act of dignity in a moment where there was none. People turned away, unable to watch. No one spoke. Not one dared disturb the king as he gathered what was left of the girl he had loved.

Corwin carried the cloak close to his chest. He walked alone, past the watchful eyes, near the outer wall, toward the southern end of the castle. There, hidden behind layers of ivy and silence, stood **the garden** his father had built in memory of his mother.

He pushed his hands through the vines that veiled the old wooden door. Leaves brushed his face, catching in his hair, as the door creaked open on rusted hinges. The garden greeted him with stillness. Sunlight filtered through arched branches overhead, dappled across wildflowers in full bloom. A bench sat beneath a weeping willow, facing a tall stone marker carved with an elegant script: *Queen Lisanna Draymoor. Beloved wife and mother. Gentle queen. May her light forever grow in the land she loved.*

Corwin knelt and laid the cloak gently beside the bench. Then he turned and left the garden without a word. He crossed the courtyard, made his way to the stables on the west end of the castle, and returned minutes later with a shovel in hand. No one stopped him. No one followed.

In the quiet of the garden, Corwin began to dig. He worked slowly. The sound of soil shifting was the only noise in the world. When the hole was finally deep enough, he knelt beside it and pulled the cloak close once more. He unwrapped it gently. Just enough to see the curve of her skull, dark, fragile, and delicate as porcelain. He smiled through tears, as if the face he remembered was still there. As if, for one last moment, she was whole.

Corwin placed her in the earth beside his mother and sat there for a while, fingers tangled in the cloak, breath catching in the still air. Then, slowly, he gathered the shovel again and returned the soil, one quiet scoop at a time, until she was in her new home.

"I am sorry," he knelt beside the fresh soil, fingers brushing the earth as if it might reach her somehow. His voice trembled. A bird called from the far edge of the garden, but Corwin barely noticed.

"I used to think being king meant power. Control. But I had neither. Not when it mattered. You changed everything. Not with swords or speeches, but with kindness and with honesty. You saw through me before I could even see myself," he swallowed hard, "you made me want to be better. For you, for the people, and for the kingdom." The wind shifted, carrying the scent of flowers and ash. He closed his eyes.

"They think I have gone mad. That I am bewitched, still under your spell. Maybe I am," he let out a shaky breath, almost laughing through the ache, "but if loving you was madness then I do not want to be sane." He stood slowly, brushing the dirt from his hands. The weight in his chest did not ease, but something in him had settled.

"I swear to you, Nyra, this kingdom will change. I will make it into the world you deserved. One where no one suffers in silence. One where no girl is ever burned for being brave," he looked down one last time.

His gaze shifted to the queen's grave. He walked over and knelt by the stone, pressing a kiss on its top, "take care of her for me, Mother," and without another word, he rose and exited the garden, leaving behind the only two people who had ever truly loved him, now resting side by side in peace.

Seventeen

Listen to Them

Corwin made his way to the castle gates and stepped beyond them, walking the worn road that led down to the village. *Her* village. The same place where he had first seen Nyra, kneeling beside that barrel of apples, too proud to cower, too kind to flinch.

As he passed through the streets, villagers had to look twice to recognize him. The polished, regal king who had marched through these roads just the day before now wandered them like a stray dog, head bowed, shoulders heavy, his royal robe stained with ash and sorrow. He reached the market square. The crowd stilled as he entered. Conversations faded into silence. Mutters followed in his wake like shadows.

He stood in the same spot where he had met her. The dirt beneath his boots felt familiar. He could almost see her kneeling there again, smiling gently as she wrapped that apple in cloth. As she told him not to kneel, not to ruin his fine clothes. Now he stood without her. And he was covered in much more than dirt.

"My people," Corwin called, voice steady despite the ache in his chest, "I ask for a moment of your time," heads turned and eyes watched, "yesterday morning, during my walk through this village, I met a girl named Nyra. She was unlike anyone I had ever met. For the first time in my life I had someone see the man before the crown.

"She opened my eyes. She showed me how blind I had been to the struggles you live with every day. She made me see how I have spent my life hiding behind gold and titles, while people like you suffered in silence. I beg your forgiveness for my ignorance. I am a man of strength not a man of experience. Just because I hold the crown to the throne does not mean it fits on my head," he paused. His voice dropped lower, more intimate.

"This kingdom is broken. It was built on the wrong values. On tradition and fear, on order above compassion. My own brother chose those values, and because of that, I lost Nyra," the silence around him deepened, "I do not wish to rule like the kings before me. I want to help you all. Nyra taught me that helping starts with listening. So let me begin there," he looked out at them, really looked.

"**Listen to them**," he could almost hear Nyra's voice in his head.

"Come forward. Speak to me. Tell me your burdens. Your hopes. Your wounds. Let me be the heart that listens to your voice," he placed a hand to his chest, "I cannot undo the past, but perhaps, with your help, I can change the future."

The people stared, wide-eyed and silent. Was this truly the king they all knew? The man who once passed through their streets on a horse draped in silk and steel, now standing in dirt and ash, face worn with grief? No one spoke, not at first. Then, an older woman stepped forward.

"I accept your apology, Your Majesty," she said quietly. Despite the rags on his shoulders and the weight in his eyes, she bowed, low and respectful. Her movements were soft, unhurried. There was no fear in her. Only grace. Something about her reminded Corwin achingly of Nyra.

"Please," he said, stepping toward her, voice gentle, "there is no need to bow to me."

Another voice broke through the hush, "do you speak the truth?" a man asked, "do you really want to change?" More muttering rose.

"I have heard nothing but empty promises from the crown my whole life," someone scoffed, "you are all liars in polished clothes."

"I think King Corwin is worth trusting," a woman spoke up from the side, "we have had more food in the past year than we have had in the last ten."

"She is right," said another, "he has done more for us than his father ever did."

"This is madness!" a man shouted, "he is royal blood. Do you really believe a king could care for a commoner?" Corwin said nothing, just listened.

Then a voice rang out, sharp and clear, "if you want us to believe you then prove it!" The square fell silent again. All eyes returned to him.

"Please," Corwin said, his voice carrying through the square, "my hands bear the blood of my own brother for what he did to Nyra. I am done hiding behind palace gates," he looked at them, really looked. Dust on his boots. Ash still in his clothes. No crown. No guards. "I want to be the king you deserve," he stood in total vulnerability.

"Then open the gates," a man called out, "tear down the walls that separate us."

Corwin paused. His whole life and education felt like it was crumbling beneath him but he nodded, his voice unwavering, "very well. The castle is open to all. There is no corner of this kingdom that will be closed to its people. No more silk screens and locked halls. No more gold for the rich while the poor go cold. Food will be evenly distributed across the land. No more priority for wealth. Stable homes and warm clothes will be guaranteed for every family. This is not just my land," he said, lifting his chin, "this is *our* land." A hush followed. The people watched him, not as a king above them, but a man standing among them.

Then, slowly, a woman stepped forward, "you have my support, King Corwin." She bowed, not out of duty, but devotion. Another followed. Then another. And another. Soon the square was full of people lowering themselves to the earth, not in fear, but in faith. They bowed to a king they could finally believe in.

An older man approached first. His hands were calloused, his clothes patched and dirty, "my son broke his leg during harvest," he said, "he has not been able to work. We barely had food last winter."

Corwin nodded, his voice low but sure, "I will send someone from the castle to your home. He will have medicine, and he will have food." The man's eyes widened. He lowered his head in quiet gratitude.

A young mother stepped forward, a child peeking shyly out from behind her skirt, "she has not had shoes in months," the woman whispered, "we could not afford them."

Corwin knelt in the dirt and smiled gently at the girl, "what's your name?"

"Emrie," she said softly.

"Well, Emrie," he said, "I may not have shoes for you today, but by tomorrow, you will have a pair warm enough to run through the snow," he looked up at her mother, "and you will have work in the kitchens, if you would like it." More came forward.

A boy who wanted to learn to read.

"The royal library holds thousands of books you can learn to read from."

A woman who had been evicted in the cold.

"You may stay in the castle until we find you a home."

A farmer who lost his land to taxes he could not pay.

"I will grant you your land back with all the means to grow whatever your heart desires."

And to each, Corwin listened. Not with empty statements, but with promises and plans.

By the time the sun dipped low on the horizon, his clothes were stained with dirt, his hands with soot, his eyes with exhaustion. But for the first time in his reign, he felt whole. As a man who had finally begun to understand what it meant to lead.

Eighteen

Agnes

The old woman who had first spoken in the square approached him again, her smile soft and kind, "Your Majesty, you look exhausted," she said, "may I make you a cup of tea?"

Corwin smiled at her gentleness. "Please, call me Corwin. And if it is no trouble, I would love some tea."

"Of course," she replied, placing a gentle hand on his arm, "come with me." She led him down the street to a modest home nestled between ivy-covered walls and old stone. It was not far, just a short walk from the market square, but for Corwin, it felt like stepping into another world.

He had spent his entire life in palaces. He had never set foot inside a commoner's home. There were no gold-plated archways. No stained glass. No chandeliers the size of tree trunks, but it was beautiful. Plants hung from ceiling hooks, sunlight filtering through their leaves. Shelves were lined with mismatched books, jars of herbs, and tiny trinkets collected over a lifetime. It was small, yes, but it felt vast in story, warm in ways stone halls never had. Then he saw it. The piano in the corner.

Its wood was worn and weathered, the keys slightly yellowed, a few chipped at the edges. His heart sank. He remembered Nyra, her fingers dancing across ivory, her music soft as snowfall. No royal musician had ever moved him the way she had.

"You like the piano?" the woman asked, setting a pot of water on the fire.

Corwin's voice dropped, heavy with memory, "I liked the girl who could play the piano," he smiled faintly, "Nyra was... incredibly talented."

The woman laughed, a light, warm sound that filled the room, "I know she was. I am the one who taught her."

Corwin blinked, stunned, "you– *you* were?"

"Yes, dear," she nodded, stirring the kettle, "she learned everything right there on that bench." She nodded toward the piano, her eyes soft with memory. Corwin turned to it again, taking it in with new awe. This was where Nyra's gift had bloomed. This was where beauty had been born from a childhood of hardship.

He looked back at the woman, "forgive me, ma'am. I never asked your name."

"**Agnes**," she said with a smile, "but Nyra always called me Annie. She had trouble pronouncing her G's when she was little." Corwin smiled, a genuine one this time. The ache in his chest did not go away, but somehow, in this quiet house, with this kind woman and that old piano, it softened.

Agnes poured the tea into a small wooden cup and handed it to him. Corwin accepted it gratefully, wrapping his hands around the warmth. He brought the cup to his lips and took a slow sip. It was warm and sweet. Sweet like...

"What's in this?" he asked softly.

"It is apple tea, dear," Agnes said, settling into her chair at the small table. She gestured for him to sit, "black tea, cinnamon, sugar, clove and apples."

Corwin paused, eyes lowering to the cup in his hands, "Nyra's apples," he whispered.

"Yes," Agnes said with a faint smile, "she returned from her aunt's orchard early yesterday, before sunrise. Brought me some and said she was heading to the market to sell the rest," she took a slow sip of her own tea, "that was the last time I saw her."

"Until I took her," Corwin murmured, setting the cup down. His stomach twisted. The warmth that once comforted him now turned bitter. He hated knowing he was the reason Agnes would never see Nyra again. If only he had not stopped. If he had ignored the apples. If he had stayed behind the guards like a proper king. But then, he would not be here. He would not have stood before the people and given them something they had never had. *Hope.*

"Do not speak like that, boy," Agnes said gently, noticing the change in his expression, "you have done nothing wrong."

"I ca not help but blame myself," Corwin sighed, his voice rough.

Agnes looked at him carefully, "what exactly happened to her?"

Corwin looked away, "she..." the words sat like thorns in his throat. He didn't want this to be what Agnes carried into her final years, a nightmare of fire and betrayal, but she deserved the truth, "she defended herself," he said slowly, "against a knight allied with my brother. Sir Ronan came to me afterward and told a twisted version of what happened. I believed Nyra. I took her side," he swallowed hard, "Darion... he could not believe I would trust the word of a servant over a knight. They decided I must have been bewitched. So they turned on me. They burned her at the stake," the words left his mouth like poison. He could barely breathe after saying them.

Agnes said nothing at first. She reached for the locket around her neck, fingers trembling as they closed around it, "ah... my dear Nyra," she whispered, voice soft, solemn, "strong to the very end."

Corwin looked at her, guilt welling in his chest again, "I am sorry..." he began.

But Agnes lifted a hand to stop him, "do not be," she said, her voice steady, "you are not the one who hurt her," she closed her eyes and held the locket tighter, grieving in silence.

"If only I had not taken her back to the castle with me..." Corwin began, voice low, but Agnes stopped him again, with a raised hand and a firm gaze.

"I already told you to stop speaking that way. You are not responsible for what happened to her," she offered a small, knowing smile, "besides, she would have made her way to you eventually, one way or another."

Corwin looked up, confused, "what do you mean?"

Agnes chuckled softly and held her hand a few feet off the ground, "she admired you since she was *this* tall. She told me, clear as day, that she was going to become a princess someday just so she could marry Prince Corwin." Heat bloomed in Corwin's cheeks. He could not help but smile. Corwin always carried the strength while Darion carried the looks. It was unusual to hear of someone falling for him over his brother.

"You were meant to meet each other," Agnes said gently, "but the world, well, it had a different ending in mind than the one you hoped for."

"It is cruel how the world will do that to you..." Corwin sighed.

"Yes, dear. I know," she replied, her voice thick with memory.

He glanced up again, "have you lost someone?"

Agnes nodded slowly, "yes, my husband and my son," her hand drifted to the locket around her neck once more.

Corwin's head bowed, "I am so sorry... May I ask what happened to them?"

Agnes did not answer right away, "they were executed. By order of your father. I tried to pull them out of the fire," with calm, steady fingers, she rolled up her sleeve to reveal a pale burn scar that curled along her forearm, "but I was dragged away. Locked in the cellar. I watched from behind iron bars as they burned."

Corwin froze. Her words hit him harder than he expected. She had lost everything to *his* family. First her husband and son to his father. And now Nyra to his brother. And even after everything, she had taken him in. Made him tea. Spoken to him like he was still worthy of forgiveness. His chest ached.

"My family has done nothing but bring harm to you," he said, voice trembling, "and yet, you trust me. You welcome me into your home. Why?"

Agnes leaned forward, her eyes soft but unwavering, "because, my dear, *you* are not your father. You are a kind man who came down to the village your ancestors trampled on and begged for forgiveness. You spoke of Nyra with love in your voice and regret in your heart. I know the kind of effect she has on people," she reached for his hand, giving it a gentle squeeze, "she changed you. And now, I am here to give you that second chance."

Corwin kept his head low. He could see now where Nyra had inherited her gentle, trusting nature. This woman had shaped her in ways he had not fully realized before.

"Would you like to play the piano?" Agnes asked, gesturing toward the worn instrument.

Corwin's eyes lit up, though a flicker of skepticism crossed his face, "play it?"

Agnes nodded with a kind smile, "yes, dear. I can teach you a simple lullaby." She rose from her chair and moved to the piano. Corwin followed, his breath catching in his throat the closer he got.

Agnes pulled out the bench for him, and he sat, feeling his heart hammer against his ribs, "this feels wrong," he muttered as she settled beside him.

"Why is that, dear?" she asked gently, placing a piece of old parchment on the music stand.

Corwin glanced at the title written across the page: *Lullay My Liking*. A common lullaby, known to both nobles and commoners. His mother had sung it to him when he was younger. His heart sank, "this is where Nyra played," he said hoarsely, "I can not sit here, not after watching her burn."

"Nonsense," Agnes said warmly, taking his hands and placing them on the keys, "music is a gift meant for all. Let the notes heal your wounds."

Corwin nodded, his fingers trembling as they rested against the worn ivory. For a moment, he did not play. He simply sat there, feeling the memory of Nyra's touch lingering on the keys. His breath came uneven, but already he could feel some of the crushing guilt loosening its hold.

"We will start with the first verse," Agnes said, pointing to the music and then to the corresponding keys, "begin with this one, E. Press it twice, as you see here."

Corwin obeyed, and at the first small sounds, a tentative smile touched his lips. The piano was not grand like the ones he had grown up with, but its voice was no less powerful. In the quiet notes, he could hear Nyra again, the way she had poured her heart into this very instrument, a memory so vivid it ached.

"Good, just like that," Agnes encouraged, "E, E, then see here? This symbol means you will move up to the black key. Then G, B, A, D, C, B. And this open note here, you hold it twice as long." Patiently, Agnes walked him through each note, one by one, until the melody began to form under his fingers like a soft thread stitching together the broken pieces of his heart.

Corwin smiled when he finally got it right. The melody came together, delicate notes weaving into a tune he recognized. Next to him, Agnes smiled too, humming softly along with his playing, *"I saw a fair maiden, Sitten and sing: She lulled a little child, a sweete Lording."*

Though her body had long surrendered to age, her voice still carried the grace of youth, pure, clear, and beautifully tender. It reminded Corwin of his mother, gentle, soothing and familiar. His heart ached, not with sorrow, but with grief. In this moment, Agnes offered him a quiet gift, the grace to begin healing.

"You have a lovely voice," he murmured, slowly lifting his hands from the keys.

"I am sure you do too," she said with a warm smile, "how about you sing with me?"

"If you ever do... sing for me..." Nyra's voice echoed in his memory.

"I do not sing," he said softly, lowering his gaze.

Agnes chuckled, "if you say so." They sat in companionable silence for a moment, the last notes of the lullaby lingering in the air like morning mist. Agnes turned her gaze to the hearth, where the fire crackled low, casting golden flickers across the stone walls.

"It is a beautiful thing, music," she said, "it knows how to find the cracks in a person. Seep in and settle."

Corwin nodded slowly, his fingers brushing the edge of the piano keys as though the music still pulsed there, "my mother used to sing it to me."

"She must have been a kind woman," Agnes said.

"She was," he said softly, "the kindest."

Agnes glanced at him, her eyes bright and knowing, "and you miss her."

"Every day," Corwin whispered.

She reached out, placing a frail, wrinkled hand over his, "we carry the ones we love in the things they left us. Songs. Sayings. Small habits we do not even notice. They are never truly gone."

Corwin looked down at their joined hands, and for a brief moment, the weight of his crown, his duty, his losses, everything felt a little lighter. He looked up and met her eyes, "thank you."

"No thanks needed, Your Majesty," she said with a small smile, "but if you ever do feel like singing, I will be here."

He gave a soft laugh, "I will keep that in mind," then he sighed as he rose to his feet, "thank you for your hospitality, but I must return to the castle."

"Of course, dear. You have a new kingdom to build," Agnes said with a knowing smile.

Corwin nodded, "I will see you again soon, Agnes. Good night."

"You as well."

He stepped out into the cool night air. The hush of the village embraced him as he paused, breathing in deeply. The scent of woodsmoke and dirt clung to the air, grounding him. As he made his way back toward the castle, his thoughts turned inward drawn to Nyra and to his mother. He missed them both, a deep ache behind every breath. Yet somehow, in Agnes's humble cottage, he had found a small piece of both of them. Her honest words, her respectful grace, the quiet warmth of her presence, it soothed something in him that was still raw.

Nineteen

What Kind of King Cries Like This?

The castle loomed ahead, its towers against the star-scattered sky. Light spilled dimly from a few high windows, flickering like distant beacons, but the rest of the great stone structure lay cloaked in shadow. It was beautiful in its own cold, imposing way, yet tonight, it felt heavier than ever.

Corwin slowed his steps as he neared the gates. The guards straightened at the sight of him, but he offered no words, just a nod. His boots crunched over gravel, each step echoing louder in the quiet. The moment he passed through the iron gate, something shifted in his chest. The warmth from Agnes's hearth seemed to fade, replaced by the chill of duty.

He stopped just inside the courtyard, letting his eyes sweep over the familiar walls. So much had changed since Nyra had arrived. Since she had smiled at him with uncertainty. Since he had dared to believe something simple and pure could exist within these walls. He drew in a long breath, the cold biting at his lungs.

"*I miss you,*" he thought, the words meant for both his mother and Nyra.

"Your Majesty!" Corwin's thoughts shattered at the sudden cry. He turned toward the voice, startled, and saw Elowyn running toward him, her face streaked with tears.

"Your Majesty," she gasped, stopping just in front of him, breathless, "is it true? Is Nyra... is she dead?" The question pierced him. Words failed. All he could manage was a single, heavy nod.

Elowyn staggered back a step, hands flying to her mouth as she trembled, "no... no, I just spoke with her last night. She was fine. Everything was fine. I– I do not understand."

Her words spiraled into frantic rambling until Corwin stepped forward and gripped her shoulders, "I know," he said quietly, "it is not fair what happened to her."

Elowyn looked up at him, eyes wide and brimming, "then why didn't you stop it?" her voice rose with each word, "why did you not do something?"

"I tried," Corwin said, his voice low but firm.

"No!" she cried, "you are the king! You should have done something! How could you let them kill an innocent girl?"

"I did not want her to die," he said, guilt tightening like a vice around his chest, "I did everything I could to protect her, but–"

"It was not enough," Elowyn cut in, voice trembling, "you let her die!" she shoved him, hard, "you monster! What kind of king are you?"

Corwin staggered back, but did not raise his voice, "please, listen to me. I wanted her alive just as much as you did. I did not give up on her, I failed her."

Elowyn shoved him again, harder, "you are supposed to protect us!"

"Elowyn–"

"No!" she struck his chest with her fists, sobbing now, "you *promised* me everyone in this castle would be safe! That we would never have to live in fear again! That you would be different!"

"ELOWYN–," Corwin said, catching her wrists gently but firmly, "I know... You have every right to be angry. I am angry too. I am broken. And I am sorry. My promises have fallen empty. I never wanted this. I do not want to rule like my father did. I *will not*. There needs to be change, Elowyn. Real change, so that what happened to Nyra never happens again, but I can not do it alone. I need your help, please."

Elowyn's expression crumpled. Her hands shook in Corwin's grasp, and her lips parted as if to argue again, but no words came. Instead, a broken sob escaped her throat.

"I am sorry," she whispered, the fight draining from her, "I am sorry, Your Majesty." She collapsed against him, burying her face in his chest as the weight of, Nyra's death, her guilt, and her grief crashed over her.

Corwin froze. For a breath, he stood still, his arms hovering in the air, unsure. Kings did not comfort crying handmaidens in open courtyards. Kings did not tremble. Kings did not *weep*. Every lesson of court and crown screamed at him to stay composed, to remain distant, to be the pillar others leaned on.

But he was not a pillar. Not tonight. He wrapped his arms around Elowyn, pulling her close, letting her grief pour into him like water into cracked stone. His eyes stung, throat tight. He wasn't sure if the tears on his cheeks were hers or his own.

"I know," he whispered into her hair, "it is all right. I know." He closed his eyes, allowing himself this small, fragile moment of humanity. His hands shook where they rested on her back. The weight of his crown had not left him, but here, in the arms of someone who should never have seen him like this, it didn't crush him quite so much. He had failed Nyra. And still, Elowyn had come to him. Had blamed him. Had cried to him. And now... now she leaned into him not as a king, but as a man. His chest ached.

What kind of king cries like this?
The kind that needed her.

When her sobs quieted to small, uneven breaths, he rested his chin gently against her head, "we can not change what happened, but we can carry her with us. We *must*."

Elowyn pulled back, just enough to look up at him. Her face was red and wet with tears, but there was something steady in her gaze now. She nodded at his words and whipped her face, "you are right. I am sorry I reacted like that, Your Majesty."

"Please," Corwin brushed her shoulders, "no more of that. Call me Corwin."

Twenty

She Deserved Everything

The two of them walked in silence through the quiet corridors of the castle. When they reached Nyra's door, Corwin paused. His hand hovered over the knob, fingers trembling. He stared at the wood grain for a long moment, like it might open by will alone. Then, slowly, he turned the handle and pushed the door open. The room was still. They stepped inside, and the silence swallowed them.

Everything remained untouched. Her cloak draped over the chair, the worn slippers at the edge of the rug, the flowers Elowyn had brought sitting quietly in a vase by the window. But it was the small tray on the bedside table that drew Elowyn forward. The food she had sent earlier was still there. The muffins, uneaten. The tea, long cold. She stared down at it, her throat tightening.

"But I will have some food sent to your room, just in case."

"You are too sweet. Thank you. Enjoy the rest of your evening."

The memory echoed in her mind, vivid and cruel in its softness. She had just wanted Nyra to feel cared for, to have something warm, something sweet. She had thought about how thin she was, how carefully she picked at her meals, like someone afraid to take more than she deserved. Now, she would never get the chance to eat those muffins.

Elowyn's lip trembled, "she never even touched them," she whispered.

Behind her, Corwin stepped slowly into the room. He let his eyes roam the space, each detail sharp and unkind. The way her bed was still made, the folded blanket at the foot of it, the faint scent of lavender still lingering in the air. He felt like an intruder in a life that had been stolen too soon.

"I thought she would have more time," he said softly, "I thought if I could just hold on long enough, if I could protect her long enough something would change. Someone would listen." He looked down, ashamed.

Elowyn turned, tears streaking silently down her cheeks, "she deserved so much more."

Corwin nodded, swallowing the lump in his throat, "**she deserved everything**."

The two of them stood in that quiet room, the ghosts of memories pressing in around them. And though there were no words that could make it right, the silence between them was shared now, grief held between two hearts, instead of one.

Corwin moved toward the small writing desk near the window, needing something to do with his hands, something to anchor himself before the grief consumed him again. Her journal sat there, closed, a worn ribbon tucked inside to mark a page. Beside it was a folded piece of parchment neatly creased. His fingers hovered over it for a moment before he gently picked it up.

There, in her handwriting, soft and curved, just a little uneven, was the title, *"Nyra's Family Apple Recipes."* His breath caught. She had told him she would write them down for him and smiled shyly when she had mentioned them. He remembered the way her eyes lit up, how proud she was to pass along something from her past. She had kept her promise, and he had not kept his.

His hand trembled as he opened the parchment. Beside each recipe, she had added little notes: *"Mama always burnt the first batch." "Use nutmeg, not cinnamon, trust me." "This one is best eaten warm, with your fingers."* Corwin closed his eyes, pressing the paper to his chest.

"She gave you a piece of her heart," Elowyn said gently. Corwin looked at the list again, fingers brushing over her handwriting as if he could feel her pulse in the ink. He sat down on the edge of her bed, the parchment still clutched tightly in his hand, one of the few pieces of her he had left. He stared at the floor, unable to speak for a moment, as the silence of her absence wrapped around him.

Elowyn sat beside him, quiet, respectful, until she finally asked, "you really loved her, didn't you?"

Corwin inhaled slowly. His chest rose with the weight of memory, "I still do," he said softly, "maybe I wasn't *in love* with her, not yet. I only knew her for a day, but in that day, she changed everything," he looked down at the parchment in his hands, the curve of her writing like a voice calling from the past.

"I feel like I am finally awake. Like I can see, *truly see*, for the first time in my life. Everything before was traditions, routines, expectations. I thought I was doing things differently than my father, but I was still following the same worn path. Still playing by the same rules," he shook his head, voice thickening.

"She opened my eyes. Not with demands or anger, not with rebellion. Just with truth. With questions. Real questions that no one else dared to ask. She did not need to raise her voice to be heard. She just *spoke,* and I listened," he paused, swallowing hard.

"She talked about the nobles and the way they treated her, about her familys loss. And still, she carried herself with such grace. Such quiet strength. Even when she had every right to rage, to accuse, to beg for justice, she did not. She remained dignified and *kind,*" his voice faltered, and he lowered his head.

"She was a beauty like no other. Not just in her face, but in the way she saw the world... in the way she made *me* see the world. And for her to be killed in such a harsh, senseless way–" his words caught in his throat, and for a long moment he could not breathe. His grip tightened around the parchment.

"She would not want you to carry the weight of her death," Elowyn said softly, "she would want you to carry what she gave you."

Corwin closed his eyes, letting the silence hold them both for a moment. Then, he spoke, calm and certain, "that is exactly what I'm going to do." They sat there in the quiet, the ghost of Nyra's presence lingering like the last note of a song.

After a beat, he turned to her, "you should go home, Elowyn. Be with your husband."

She hesitated, concern flickering in her eyes, "are you going to be alright?"

He gave a small nod, gaze distant but steady, "yes. I will be. Please… go be with him tonight. We will see each other soon."

Elowyn lingered a second longer before rising slowly from the bed. She gave his arm a gentle squeeze, then walked quietly to the door. Corwin remained a moment longer, the weight of the paper still warm in his hand, her handwriting, her memory, her quiet strength. Then he stood, following her out. He paused at the doorway, glanced once more at the room behind him, and stepped into the hall.

Twenty One

Are You There?

Corwin walked back to his room, moving through the castle in silence. The place he had always called home had never felt so foreign. In his chambers, he carefully removed his robes, the ones that held Nyra's ashes, Darion's blood, and Elowyn's tear, and changed into his night attire. His eyes lingered on the robes now lying across his bed, the very same ones he had worn when she died. He could not bear to wash them, could not bring himself to cast them away. Instead, he folded them neatly and placed them on top of the wardrobe.

He laid down and stared at the ceiling. His mind spiraled through the chaos of the past few days. It felt as if the ground beneath him had been ripped away. He closed his eyes, but all he could see was her. Her face. Her screams. Her burning silhouette. He tossed and turned, haunted, before finally rising and heading into the bathroom. From a cupboard, he opened a small chest and retrieved a delicate glass vial.

"*Chamomile, lavender, and lemon,*" his mother's voice echoed softly in his memory, "*will put even the most playful puppy to sleep.*"

He took a slow sip, letting the sweet, familiar taste coat his throat. Warmth spread through his chest, part nostalgia, part sorrow. He returned to bed and curled beneath the covers. Humming softly, he sang the lullaby his mother used to soothe him with, the same melody

Agnes had taught him again on the piano. His voice was barely more than a whisper. Sleep was coming quickly until he heard a knock.

Corwin stirred, blinking into the darkness, "enter," he called groggily. The door creaked open. He squinted, trying to make out the figure standing there.

"Your Majesty?" a familiar voice said.

He sat up, grabbing the candle from his bedside table and lifting it toward the face. As the flickering light met the figure, Corwin gasped and dropped the candle. It landed at his feet, the flame extinguished on impact.

He stumbled back. "*Nyra!?*"

"Your Majesty, **are you there?**" she asked again, her voice tender but distant.

Corwin's heart pounded and his hands trembled, "how are you here?"

"You left me," Nyra whispered, "I came back to find you."

She stepped closer. He reached out, desperate to feel her. To make her real, but when his fingers met her arm, there was no soft skin. Instead he was only met with ash. It sifted through his hand like sand, weightless and cold. Panic surged through him.

"Nyra," he breathed. He reached for her again, but in an instant, she burst into flames.

"Corwin? Corwin, are you still there?" she sobbed, the fire curling around her like chains.

"I am here! Do not worry, I am here!" Corwin cried, lunging forward, but the more he reached, the farther she drifted. He ran, desperate and useless. Until all that remained was a pile of ash. He dropped to his knees beside it, tears falling freely.

"No, Nyra... please. I tried– I tried to save you, but you were too far away..." he cradled the ash in his hands, sobbing as it mixed with his tears.

"Corwin? Corwin, why did you leave me?"

He turned. Nyra stood behind him, not as he remembered. Her body was burned and broken, her eyes hollow pits. Corwin stumbled backward, his breath caught in his throat.

"I did not leave you," he pleaded, "I never meant for any of this to happen."

"You left me to die," she said, voice cracking, "after you promised to protect me. You are full of empty truths and broken promises," she cried, blackened tears streaking her ruined face, "you are just like your father."

"Please," Corwin begged.

She raised a flaming hand, "and now... it is your turn to burn."

Corwin screamed and ran. The world around him twisted into a field of smoke and flame. She followed him, fire rising with every step she took. The sound of knocking echoed in the distance. Louder. Louder. Louder–

Corwin sat bolt upright in bed, gasping for air. Sweat clung to his skin. The knocking was real now, persistent and urgent. Someone was at his door.

"Your Majesty?"

Corwin jolted at the voice and ran a hand over his damp face, wiping away the sweat clinging to his brow, "enter," he croaked.

The door creaked open, and a guard peeked in, eyes wide with unease. "Your Majesty... There are thousands of villagers at the castle gates. They are demanding entry."

Corwin blinked, trying to shake off the remnants of his nightmare. Then he remembered the speech, the promise, his call for change. They had come.

"Let them in," he said without hesitation.

The guard hesitated, "but, Sire–"

"I said let them in," Corwin snapped, his voice firm and final, "do you understand?"

The guard straightened, bowing quickly, "right away, Your Majesty."

Twenty Two

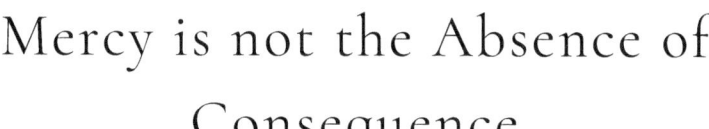

Mercy is not the Absence of Consequence

Corwin quickly dressed and rushed outside, his heart still pounding from the nightmare. As he reached the outer courtyard, a line of guards stood firm at the castle gates, weapons drawn, barring the path of a swelling crowd beyond.

"Open the gates!"

"Let us in!"

"He promised!"

"We want to speak to the king!"

Shouts rose in a storm of desperation and hope. The villagers pressed closer, voices thick with urgency, but the guards remained still, braced for resistance. Corwin pushed through the line of armor and steel, stepping in front of his men.

"Open the gates," he commanded.

One of the guards stepped forward, "Your Majesty, I must advise against this. It is not a wise decision."

"You do not make the decisions," Corwin said, voice hard, "open the gate." The guards glanced at one another, unease rippling through the line. No one moved.

Then finally, one guard gave a small nod and stepped toward the gate, "right away, Sire."

The heavy doors creaked open, and the crowd surged forward, not in a riot, but in a wave of stunned disbelief. Some rushed with joy, some lingered at the threshold, hesitant. But they came with something new in their eyes. *Hope.*

A guard approached Corwin's side, leaning in close, "forgive me, Your Majesty," he said under his breath, "but I urge you to reconsider."

"And why is that?" Corwin asked, eyes fixed on the flood of people entering the courtyard.

"They are villagers, commoners. They are greedy, and unpredictable. Some will steal, others might turn violent. They are a threat to everything inside these walls."

Corwin turned to him slowly, his gaze sharpening, "and what makes you say that?"

The guard sneered, nodding toward the crowd, "just look at them. Filthy. Undisciplined. There is a reason they are beneath us."

Corwin's face darkened. He snatched the spear from the guard's grip with one swift motion, "you will show them respect. These are my people, and they matter to me as much as you do. Lineage does not hold meaning here, not anymore."

The guard scoffed, "lineage means nothing? Do you hear yourself?"

Corwin stepped in close, voice low but cutting, "yes, and so will you, or you may leave this place and never return."

The guard fell silent under Corwin's piercing glare. Without another word, he slipped back into line stripped of his spear and his pride.

Corwin turned to the gathering crowd and stepped forward, his voice calm but strong, "the Draymoor castle is no longer a place of separation," he declared, "but a place of unity. Here, we are equals regardless of blood or birth. You are free to roam these halls. No doors are barred to my people."

A mutter of awe rippled through the villagers until a sharp scream tore through the peace, "he is dead! Prince Darion is dead!" Ronan came stumbling into the courtyard, his face pale, bandages still wrapped around his head where Nyra had struck him. Gasps echoed through the crowd as all eyes snapped to him.

"Ronan," Corwin said, lifting a hand to calm him, "please, contain yourself."

"Your brother is dead, and you tell me to *contain myself?*" Ronan bellowed, his voice cracking with rage, "you killed him, didn't you?"

The courtyard fell silent. The air turned heavy and tight. All sound, all movement, seemed to vanish. Hundreds of eyes locked on Corwin. He stood still, exposed, but not shaken.

"Darion was already lost," Corwin said slowly, carefully, "I did not kill a prince, I killed a monster."

"A monster?" Ronan's voice was bitter, disbelieving, "the only monster here is *you*, for raising your sword against your own blood!"

Corwin stepped forward, anger flaring in his chest, "Darion cared for nothing but power. His heart was poisoned by greed. He would have watched this kingdom burn just to rule over its ashes. He took the life of an innocent girl, a girl *you* assaulted!"

A fresh wave of gasps broke out among the crowd. Whispers began to spread like wildfire. Ronan's expression darkened, his eyes holding no guilt.

"She was a servant, nothing more," Ronan hissed.

Corwin clenched his fists, "she was more than any title you ever held. This kingdom will never again excuse cruelty under the name of rank or tradition."

Ronan's eyes shifted past Corwin to the guards behind him, "do you hear this?" he called out, "your king has *fallen!*" The guards exchanged uncertain glances. Doubt rippled through their ranks like a spreading crack.

Corwin stepped forward, voice steady, unwavering, "I have not fallen, I have *grown*. Grown beyond this poisoned tradition that treats the people of this land as if they are less than human. That ends now."

He turned to face the crowd, lifting his voice, "this castle was built on the backs of the people. It is time they step through its gates not as beggars, but as builders." A wave of murmurs surged through the villagers. Then, scattered claps. Cheers. A few raised their hands in the air, the spark of hope catching fire.

Ronan's face twisted in rage, "cut this *nonsense* at once! You are not a child anymore, Corwin. You are a king! It is time you start acting like one. There is no place for dreams in the throne room. You have a duty to fulfill!"

Corwin's jaw tightened. He stepped closer to Ronan, his voice low and cutting, "I *am* fulfilling it. My duty is not to uphold cruelty and call it tradition. My duty is to serve this kingdom and all who live in it."

Ronan drew his sword with a sharp metallic hiss, "I will not let Darion's memory be disgraced like this," he growled.

Corwin tightened his grip on the spear, stepping forward with controlled calm, "I do not wish for bloodshed, Ronan. Not here. This is a place of peace now. Lay down your weapon or walk away."

Ronan's eyes burned with fury, "you will have to *kill me* to make me leave." He raised his sword, stalking closer. The steel glinted in the morning sun like a challenge.

Without a word, several guards stepped away from Corwin's side and moved beside Ronan, their blades drawn. The shift was subtle, but the betrayal echoed loudly in the silence. Corwin looked around, he was encircled. No armor. No shield. Just a single spear and the weight of his conviction. His heart pounded, but he stood firm.

"So this is how you honor the crown," he said, his voice like stone, "with steel against your king." The crowd watched in stunned silence, waiting to see what would happen next.

"Corwin, someday you will be king," his father said to him, "you will have to be prepared for anything and everything. There will come a day where your life will become like a valuable gem. Everyone will want to steal it. You need to learn to defend yourself even in the most impossible situations."

"Father, I do not want to fight," Corwin began.

"Silence my boy. Fighting is crucial for a king. If you can not fight, you can not rule," he picked up a fake sword.

"Where is my sword?" Corwin asked.

"You do not get one. You have to learn how to fight defenseless." A few knights joined the king's side.

"Father, I can not fight multiple men without a weapon," Corwin backed away in fear.

"Not yet. You will learn."

Corwin held his spear tight, "I am begging, please, no more bloodshed."

"Then surrender, Corwin," Ronan closed in on him, "you can not win against twenty armed men."

"It is simple really, do not let the sword touch you," the king swung his fraud weapon. Corwin quickly ducted, effectively dodging the attack.

"Father, please, I do not want to do this," Corwin begged again. He tried to run but ran into a knight who also swung at him.

"You underestimate my abilities. I received triple the training Darion did," Corwin grounded himself to the stone beneath him.

"Fight Corwin! Fight! You can not dodge forever!"

Ronan's lips twisted in a cruel smile, "you may be strong but you are not a God. One man can not take down an army."

"Just like that Corwin! Faster! Do not let your guard down!"

"I will protect my people at all cost, even if that means doing the impossible," Corwin's brow furrowed.

Ronan laughed, "just like you protected that servant girl?"

"Can you feel that Corwin? The rage? The fire surging through your veins? Let it take over. Let your heart lend you its strength."

Corwin swung his spear and suddenly a wave of steel came charging toward him. Corwin's grip on the spear tightened as the circle of steel closed in. The guards did not wait for commands this time, they surged forward all at once.

The first three came together from the front. Corwin pivoted, ducking under the nearest sword and driving the butt of his spear into the gut of one man, knocking him back into the others. He spun in a tight arc, slashing the spear's blade across a guard's chestplate, the force knocking the man flat.

"Chin up!"

There was no time to breathe. A blade hissed from behind. Corwin twisted just in time, catching the glint in the corner of his eye. He dropped to one knee as the sword missed his neck and whirled his spear like a wheel, sweeping the legs out from two soldiers behind him. As they hit the ground, he planted the spear like a lever and hurdled into the air, twisting midair and landing hard on one of the fallen men, elbow cracking into his jaw.

"Surround him!" Ronan barked.

Four more came at once. One slashed high, Corwin raised the shaft to block. Another stabbed low, he twisted to avoid it, but a third guard slammed a shield into his ribs, knocking the wind from him. Corwin staggered back, sweat flying from his hair, blood trailing down his lip.

"Focus, Corwin, focus! Be aware of your surroundings, all three hundred sixty degrees."

He used his spear like a scythe now, slicing horizontally to keep the group back. When one tried to counter, Corwin stepped into him, gripped the shaft like a quarterstaff, and spun, cracking the man across the temple. The guard fell limp.

"Father, my arm hurts, I can not keep going!"

"You have other parts of your body, use them."

Another grabbed his arm. Corwin slammed his head back, breaking the man's nose with a crunch, then slammed his boot into a kneecap with enough force to drop him screaming. A sword grazed his back. He winced, but did not slow. His body was a blur of movement. Every part of him was weaponized. Elbows, knees, feet, fists.

Someone lunged. Corwin caught the man's wrist mid-strike, flipped him over his shoulder, and sent him crashing into two others. Now bloodied, bruised, and heaving, Corwin stood in the center of a pile of groaning bodies. His eyes were wild, chest rising and falling like a war drum. Ronan stood at the edge of the massacre, trembling with rage, sword still drawn but unmoving.

"Who else wants to test my resolve?" Corwin shouted, his voice echoing through the courtyard. The remaining guards looked at each other uncertainly. Some lowered their swords. Some even stepped back.

Corwin pointed the spear at Ronan, eyes burning, "this ends now."

The tension broke like a snapped bowstring. Ronan roared and charged, sword raised high. Corwin steadied his stance, planting his feet in the blood-slick stone as the knight came at him like a storm. Steel clashed. Spear against sword. Sparks flew. The courtyard lit with the rhythm of violence. The crowd was silent, breathless.

"You call yourself king," Ronan snarled, swinging hard. Corwin blocked, the force reverberating down his arms.

"I am king," Corwin snapped, countering with a sweep of his spear. Ronan jumped back, barely avoiding the blade.

"No true king abandons his blood for a servant girl!"

"No true prince murders in cold blood!"

Ronan lunged, jabbing for Corwin's heart. Corwin twisted, the tip grazing his side. He grunted, then twisted his spear up, catching Ronan under the chin with the wooden end and staggering him back.

"She was nothing!" Ronan spat, recovering fast, fury in his every movement.

"She was everything I was too blind to see!" Corwin struck again, forcing Ronan to retreat with a flurry of precise, punishing strikes.

"You betrayed your people for her!"

"I *saved* my people from what we were becoming!" Corwin's next swing knocked Ronan's sword from his grip, but Ronan was not done. He rushed Corwin barehanded, tackling him to the ground. They rolled across the stones, trading punches, grappling like wolves in the dirt.

"You are weak," Ronan hissed, trying to choke him, blood trickling from his nose, "you have lost your edge."

"No," Corwin growled, pushing back with raw force, their faces inches apart, "I have finally found my strength." He twisted free, grabbed the spear, and rolled to his feet. Ronan rose too, snatching a fallen sword.

"You will die with your ideals," Ronan panted, circling.

"Then I will die a better man than you."

They collided one last time, sword and spear clashing in a blur. Corwin ducked a wild swing, drove the butt of the spear into Ronan's knee. The knight cried out and dropped. Corwin pressed the spearpoint to his throat. Ronan froze, chest heaving.

"Do it," he snarled, "finish what you started." Corwin's arms trembled. The crowd waited.

"No," he said softly, "this kingdom has seen enough death." He stepped back, lowering the spear. Ronan looked up, hatred simmering, but he did not move.

Corwin turned to the crowd, bloodied, bruised, breath ragged, but before a word could leave his mouth, searing pain exploded through his leg. A blade had pierced his calf. He collapsed to one knee with a cry, the world tilting for a moment.

"You are pathetic, Corwin," Ronan's voice slithered through the silence. He barely laid upright on the ground, blood leaking from his mouth, "your father would be ashamed to see what you have become." Corwin's eyes flared. With a grunt, he kicked Ronan hard in the jaw. Bone cracked.

"Do not speak of my father in such a way," Corwin snarled. With trembling fingers, he gripped the hilt of the sword embedded in his leg. He let out a hoarse, guttural scream as he yanked it free. Blood gushed. He staggered to his feet, leaning on the weapon like a crutch, pain radiating up his spine. But he stood tall. He limped over, his shadow falling over Ronan's broken form. With grim finality, Corwin stomped down on the knight's hands, pinning his arms to the stone.

"It is time you learned respect," he lifted the sword.

Ronan coughed, a bloody smirk on his cracked lips, "I thought you were sparing me, *Your Majesty*."

"I am," Corwin said, "but **mercy is not the absence of consequence**."

He looked into Ronan's eyes, not with hate. Nyra had taught him better. Hate would only rot the soul. This was not vengeance he sought, it was balance. Corwin raised the blade high, gripping it with both hands, and in one clean stroke he brought it down. Ronan's scream echoed through the courtyard, raw and feral as blood sprayed across the stone.

"For touching her," Corwin said coldly, tossing the sword aside, "for violating what was never yours." Ronan writhed, cradling the stumps where his hands once were, sobbing curses between gurgling gasps. Corwin turned his gaze back to the crowd.

His leg shook beneath him, blood dripping from his wound, but his voice came steady, "no more kings who rule with fear. No more silence for the powerless. Today marks a new beginning." The villagers erupted into cheers, a thunderous roar rising with the wind. Some wept. Some knelt. Others reached through the crowd just to touch the steps he stood on. As the sunlight broke through the clouds overhead, Corwin stood, not just a king, but a man reborn.

But the toll on his body could no longer be ignored. Corwin took a step forward, and then another, before the world around him spun in a dizzying swirl of color. The cheers of the villagers warped and faded, like echoes underwater. His grip on reality loosened.

The pain, the blood loss, the weight of all he had fought for it caught up to him all at once. His knees buckled, and before another soul could catch him, King Corwin Draymoor collapsed at the foot of his own castle, surrounded by the corpses of the men who once pledged loyalty to his crown.

Twenty Three

Do I Have to be King?

"Your Majesty? Your Majesty, can you hear me?" a voice called, distant and muffled, like it came through water. Corwin groaned, trying to open his eyes. Pain radiated through his body, sharp, electric, and relentless.

"Your Majesty," the voice said again, more clearly now, "my name is Elis. I am a doctor. You collapsed after the battle with the guards. You lost a significant amount of blood, but I managed to stop the bleeding."

Battle. Yes. The fight. The gates. Ronan. Another groan escaped him as he shifted slightly. Every muscle screamed in protest. He could hear the sound of someone moving beside him. Finally, with great effort, Corwin forced his eyes open. An older man hovered at his bedside, his expression calm but concerned.

"Elis..." Corwin rasped, "I can not feel my leg."

The doctor's face darkened with quiet regret, "I am sorry, Your Majesty. The wound was deep, and you were bleeding out. I had to act quickly. I tied a cloth tightly to stop the flow. But... without circulation for so long, the tissue has decayed." Elis gently pulled back the sheet. Corwin stared. His leg lay limp and discolored, spotted in deep reds and purples. It looked foreign and useless and raggedy.

"Is there no saving it?" he asked, voice hollow.

"I am afraid not," Elis said gently, silence settled thick between them, "I wanted to wait until you woke before moving forward."

"Moving forward?" unease settled in Cowrin's stomach.

Elis nodded, "your leg is no longer of use to you. It would be best to sever it from your body to reduce further complications."

Corwin swallowed hard, uncomfortable with the situation. He looked down at his decaying limb, "very well."

"I will begin the procedure tomorrow, you must rest for now," then, Elis raised a small cup to Corwin's lips, "drink."

Corwin took a sip and immediately choked. He turned his face away, coughing, "what *is* that?"

"Wheatgrass and alfalfa. To help rebuild your blood. The taste is… unpleasant, I know, but you must drink it." Corwin winced, his jaw tight, but he took the cup and forced the rest down. Each swallow was a challenge, but he did not stop. He had endured worse.

When he finished, he leaned back against the pillows, chest heaving. His body ached. He wanted nothing more than to go to sleep and wake up in his mothers lap, humming a sweet tune as she embroidered.

*"Mama… **do I have to be king?**" Corwin clung to the fabric of her dress. The fire crackled nearby, casting a soft golden light across the royal chambers.*

His mother stroked his hair gently, humming a tune only she knew, "one day, yes, but not today."

"I do not want to. What if I am not strong enough? What if I ruin everything?"

She smiled down at him, "you think being strong means never being afraid?"

He looked up at her, eyes wet, "does it not?"

"No," she whispered, brushing a strand of hair behind his ear, "being strong means standing back up, even when you are afraid. It means choosing kindness when anger is easier. And it means loving your people so deeply, you would carry their burdens on your back, even when your legs give out."

"I do not think I can do that."

"You will," she said, kissing his forehead, "because you were born with a heart that aches for others. That is a rare strength, my boy, and one day, it will make you a king unlike any other."

"Your Majesty, I have brought a cane for you in case you need to get up," Elis said gently, setting the polished wood cane beside the bed.

"Thank you, Elis," Corwin replied with a tired nod.

"Is there anything else I can do for you at the moment?"

Corwin hesitated, then said, "just one thing... Call me Corwin."

Elis paused, clearly unused to such an informal request, but he offered a warm smile, "as you wish. I will be nearby. Just ring the bell if you need anything."

Corwin let his head fall back onto the pillow. Despite the rest, his body still felt like lead. His leg throbbed beneath the blanket. He hated the helplessness. Hated feeling useless. A soft knock came at the door.

"Enter," he called.

The door creaked open, and a young boy stepped inside. He had dark curls, a curious gaze, and a small wooden box under one arm, "King Corwin?"

Corwin managed a smile, "hello, young one. Can I help you with something?"

"Actually... I came to see if I could help *you*," the boy said, stepping further into the room, "my grandfather is Elis, the man who has been tending to your injuries. He told me what happened... about your leg."

Corwin's smile faded. He shifted uncomfortably and pulled the blanket a little higher over the discolored limb, "yes. It seems it will not be working again."

"I lost my leg too," the boy said matter-of-factly, lifting his pant leg, "a horse carriage ran over me a couple years ago. Took it clean off. So I built this," He tapped his wooden prosthetic, "I have made lots. I have to build a new one every few months since I keep growing."

Corwin leaned forward, impressed, "you made that yourself?"

The boy grinned, "I sure did."

"You are quite a resourceful young man."

"I was wondering if you would like me to make you one," he said, stepping closer to the bed with hopeful eyes.

Corwin blinked, "make me one?"

"Yes, Your Majesty," the boy replied proudly.

Corwin gave a small chuckle, warmed by the offer, "I would be honored. But no more 'Your Majesty.' I do not wish to be addressed by my title."

The boy nodded quickly, "right. Corwin. May I take your measurements?"

"Please," Corwin said, adjusting his leg so the boy could reach. As the child pulled a worn tape measure from his box and began working carefully, Corwin watched him with growing admiration, "what is your name, boy?"

"Samric," he said with a smile, "but most people call Sam."

"It is very nice to meet you Sam," Corwin said.

"You as well Your Maje– uh... Corwin. Sorry force of habit," he grinned sheepishly. Sam finished taking his measurement and packed his things, "I will have that to you by tomorrow."

"Thank you, truly."

"Of course," and with that he left the room. As the door closed behind Sam, silence settled over the room once more. A wooden leg. Crafted by a boy no older than ten, who had known pain, loss, and yet maintained his resilience and pride. There was a quiet strength in Samric that stirred something deep in Corwin's chest.

He looked down at his own bandaged leg, useless now, but no longer a mark of shame. It was a symbol. A scar of choice, of defiance, of change. His mind drifted to Nyra's words, still echoing like a heartbeat in the chambers of his memory.

"Listen to them."

He closed his eyes. The ache in his body remained, but the weight on his heart felt lighter. Corwin Draymoor would walk again, maybe not with the same stride as before, but with a new purpose. One carved from pain, tempered by love, and carried forward by the very people he once thought himself above.

Twenty Four

It is Gone

The next morning brought a soft knock at the door. Corwin, propped up against his pillows, turned his head, "enter."

Samric stepped in, clutching a bundle wrapped in cloth, his eyes bright with excitement, "I finished it."

Corwin couldn't help but smile, "you are a boy of your word."

Samric walked over and gently placed the bundle on the edge of the bed, "it is not perfect," he said, unwrapping the cloth, "but it is strong. Oak wood, polished and sealed. I even carved a bit of the castle crest into the side." He pulled back the last layer to reveal the leg. It was simple, sturdy, and surprisingly elegant in its craftsmanship. Corwin stared at it, speechless.

Corwin reached out and ran his fingers over the smooth wood. "It's beautiful."

"Once Papa finishes the procedure, all you have to do is strap this garter above your knee and hook it into the leather straps here," Sam explained, pointing to the careful assembly of belts and buckles, "you are lucky you still have your knee. I lost mine when the carriage hit me."

Corwin's eyes lingered on the leg for a moment, then drifted to the boy's face, "I am forever in your debt for this."

Samric shook his head, "that is not necessary. I am just doing what any good man would do."

Corwin smiled softly, but with a flicker of rekindled joy in his chest, "then you are already more of a man than many I have known." A soft knock stirred the quiet of the chamber.

"Come in," Corwin called, bracing himself. The door creaked open, and Elis stepped in, his weathered face calm but heavy with the weight of what had to be done. A tray of sterilized instruments rested in his hands, wrapped in linen.

"It is time," Elis said gently. Corwin swallowed hard and nodded. He looked down at his leg still, purpled, and lifeless beneath the sheets. It did not even feel like it was his anymore. Just a burden attached to him by memory. Samric stepped back from the bed, respectfully quiet, his wooden leg cradled in his arms like a gift waiting for rebirth.

"I will be just outside," the boy said, offering Corwin a reassuring look before slipping out the door.

Elis approached and set the tray down, "this will be painful, but I have prepared a serum to dull your nerves. You will drift, but you may still feel flashes."

"I am not afraid," Corwin whispered, though his clenched fists said otherwise.

"You have already faced death and survived. This is just another step toward healing." Elis poured a bitter-smelling liquid into a small clay cup and handed it to him, "drink."

Corwin brought it to his lips. The taste was earthy and sharp, stinging all the way down. Almost immediately, the edges of the world began to blur. Light shimmered oddly. The pain in his leg faded to a distant throb.

"Lie back," Elis instructed, unrolling his tools with the precision of a man who had done this more times than he wished. Corwin leaned into the pillow, his breath slowing. The ceiling seemed far away.

Elis placed a firm hand on Corwin's thigh, "I will make it quick. Focus on something good." Corwin's mind drifted, not to battles or bloodshed, but to a quiet memory. Nyra's piano playing. The way she sucked the darkness out of the room and made a melody like he had never heard before. The first cut was made. Then everything went quiet.

The first thing he felt was the weight of absence. A cold emptiness where part of him used to be. Corwin's eyes blinked open slowly. Sunlight filtered through the curtains, soft and golden, casting lines across the ceiling. For a moment, he was not sure where he was. Then the ache returned, dull and deep, radiating from his knee. He turned his head.

Elis sat in a chair by the bedside, writing something down, his hands still stained faintly with dried blood. Corwin shifted slightly. He did not cry out, but his breath staggered. Instinctively, he reached down under the blanket. His hand met bandages... and nothing beyond them. It was real.

"Elis..." he whispered.

The older man stirred immediately, "Corwin. You are awake."

Corwin nodded slowly, "**it is gone**."

"Yes," Elis said gently, placing a hand on his shoulder.

Corwin stared at the ceiling for a long moment, the silence heavy between them, "it feels strange. Like... it should still be there."

"That is natural. The mind clings to what the body can no longer hold," he stood, walking to the table to pour water into a clay cup, "here, sip slowly."

Corwin accepted it with trembling hands, "did I say anything while I was under?"

"You whispered a name," Elis said quietly, "Nyra."

Corwin shut his eyes, "of course I did." Elis said nothing, only placed a comforting hand on his arm. A knock broke the stillness.

"Enter," Corwin said, his voice steadier this time. The door creaked open, and Samric entered, cradling the polished wooden leg in both arms. His gaze flicked to the bed, to the empty space where Corwin's leg used to be, but he did not look away or grimace. Instead, he approached with quiet confidence and offered the prosthetic.

Corwin accepted it carefully, his fingers tracing over the smooth grain. It was beautifully crafted, lightweight, balanced, and shaped with care. He strapped the garter around his thigh just as Samric had instructed, then slipped the nub of his limb into the socket. The leather straps were supple but strong, fastening securely across his leg.

He bent his knee experimentally. The weight shifted in a way that surprised him. It was stable, supportive, almost natural. It was strange not to feel his leg, but it did not feel wrong. Just... different.

"I can teach you how to walk with it, if you would like," Samric said, a proud smile tugging at his lips. Corwin gave him a grateful nod and slowly swung his legs over the edge of the bed. The cold floor met his bare foot as he sat up straight, bracing himself. He took a deep breath and pushed himself up. A grunt escaped him as he stood, the pressure flared through the bandaged stump, and his muscles trembled from the effort.

"You may have to use the cane for a few weeks as the amputation heals," Elis said, stepping in to steady him, "take it slow. Your body is still adjusting." Corwin gritted his teeth but stayed standing. He grasped the cane with one hand and took a cautious step. The wooden leg met the floor with a dull tap. Another step. Then another.

Samric stood back, watching with a smile, "you are doing great."

Corwin let out a breath, half a laugh, half a sigh, "it is not graceful... but it is progress."

"You will get there," Samric said, "you just took your first steps as a new man."

Corwin glanced down at the leg, then back up at the boy, "I feel like a kid again, learning how to walk for the first time."

Samric laughed, "it is a funny feeling, isn't it?."

Corwin nodded, "I thank you both deeply for everything you have done."

Elis bowed, "it is my honor."

Twenty Five

Call me Corwin

Corwin took another step. Then another. The pain was sharp, but it was not greater than his will. He adjusted the cane in his grip, grounding himself. "I think I am ready," he said, glancing toward Elis and Samric, "I need to speak to them, everyone."

"To the villagers?" Elis asked.

Corwin nodded, "they deserve to hear the truth from me, not whispers from frightened mouths or bloodied stone."

Elis placed a steadying hand on his shoulder, "then let us get you dressed Corwin."

A short while later, Corwin stepped into the crisp morning light, his cloak draped over his shoulders and the cane thudding softly against the stone as he moved. Samric trailed beside him, ready to catch him if he lost his balance. His steps were slow and deliberate, but firm.

As he emerged into the courtyard, whispers spread like wind through the gathered crowd. The villagers had already assembled, drawn by word of his survival, his battle, his fall. As the remaining guards gathered them around, Corwin raised a hand to still them. He stood tall despite the ache in his body and the wooden leg beneath him.

"My people," he called, voice ringing through the square, "I stand before you not as a king untouched by pain, but as a man who has bled for this land. I have made mistakes. I have allowed darkness to make its way into these walls." The crowd fell into silence, all eyes on him.

"I have lost much, but in that loss, I have remembered who I am meant to be. Not a ruler of fear, but a guardian of peace. I vow to rebuild what has been broken. I vow to listen. To protect and to serve. I do not ask for blind loyalty. I ask for your hands, your hearts, and your honesty," he looked over the men, women, children, their faces marked by grief, uncertainty, and hope.

"Yes, I killed my brother and those guards," Corwin said, his voice steady but thick with sorrow, "but I do not wish to rule by blood. I wish to build a land of peace. One not ruled by a single man, but shaped by the will of all who live in it."

A heavy silence settled before an older man stepped forward, eyes narrowed, "you say that now, but where were you when we needed you most? When the plague swept through our homes and left our beds cold? When winter froze our bones and the castle fires burned high while we starved outside?"

Before Corwin could answer, a woman strode forward and shoved the man aside, "that plague was during his father's rule, and you know it. King Corwin has done more in one year than the old king did in his lifetime. This is our chance for something better. Do not ruin it with bitterness."

Another voice joined her, " she is right. When was the last time you heard a king *beg* his people for forgiveness?"

A scoff came from the crowd, "he is still a king. Can we *really* trust him?"

"Oh for the love of the gods," someone shouted, "we watched him fight a whole army of his own men because they disrespected us. If that does not speak for his character, I do not know what does."

"I do not want my children to grow up the way I did," a young mother added, holding her daughter close, "cold, afraid, and unheard. If King Corwin can change that, then he has my loyalty."

The people murmured in agreement, their voices rising like the wind over the stone courtyard. There was a rich tension in the air, still uncertain and scarred, but time and time again, Corwin had proven himself. Not through achievements or gold, but through humility, action, and sacrifice. He stood silently as they spoke among themselves, choosing not to command, but to listen. Letting the voice of the people rise. Letting them shape the world they longed for.

"Your Majesty," a woman with a kind smile stepped forward, "I can read and write in several languages. Perhaps... I could start a school?"

"I want to learn how to read!" a little boy piped up, running toward her.

"Me too! Me too!" more children joined, their faces alight with curiosity.

"If anyone wants to cook, I would be happy to teach," said Elowyn, stepping beside Corwin and resting a hand on his shoulder.

"I can teach woodworking!" Samric chimed in proudly, knocking on his wooden leg with a grin.

"I can help too," another added, "if I had more materials, I could build tools or even houses."

"I sew," said a woman twirling in a vibrant, hand-stitched dress, "all kinds of clothes for all kinds of people."

"I can garden."

"I can clean."

"I'm good with animals."

"My papa can teach medicine!" Samric beamed, throwing an arm over Elis's shoulder, nearly knocking him over. Laughter trickled through the crowd, warm and real. One by one, they stepped forward not to beg, but to offer.

Corwin stood back, watching. He said nothing as the people came together, hand in hand, voice by voice, to create something new. For the first time since Nyra's death, Corwin smiled. Not the smile he wore in court. Not the strained smile of survival, but genuine. Something buried deep within his soul rising like sunlight after a long, cruel storm.

Then, a man with a dirt-streaked face and a worn pickaxe stepped boldly to the front, "if you want us to *really* believe in you," he said, grinning, "then tear down the walls. Not just opening the gates, *smash* them. Turn the stone to dust!" He raised his pickaxe high as a cheer followed behind him.

Corwin nodded, no hesitation in his eyes, "if that's what you wish. No more walls between us. No more titles separating us. No more burdens binding us. From this day forward, we build together."

He turned, motioning toward the castle. "The library is open to read and to teach. The kitchen is open to cook and to share. The workshops, the gardens, the stables, the apothecary, all of it is yours. Seren will help you find fabrics and supplies. Samric and Elis can lead the carpenters and medics. Every skill, every hand, every heart will grow with each other."

Then, without ceremony, Corwin stepped down from the platform and into the crowd walking as a man, as one of them.

"And please," he said, smiling at the sea of faces before him, "**call me Corwin**."

Twenty Six

I am Not You

The man with the pickaxe let out a triumphant shout and ran toward the palace wall. Others followed with tools, all with purpose in their eyes. Pickaxes, hammers, chisels, whatever they could find. The first crack of stone echoed through the courtyard.

The ancient walls that had stood as symbols of separation, of power and distance, began to crumble under the will of the people. Dust filled the air, but no one flinched. Laughter rang out, cheers burst forth, and for the first time in living memory, the palace and the village beat as one heart.

Corwin smiled faintly, watching it all unfold. The birth of something new, carved out of the ruin of the old. Quietly, he turned away. He slipped through the side door near the garden arch. No one followed as he climbed the spiral staircase, each step echoing through the silent upper halls. He walked through corridors he had known all his life, corridors that felt older now, colder. Finally, he reached the door to the chapel. He pushed it open and stepped inside.

The air was still. Beams of pale light filtering through the stained glass. Everything was as it had always been, too polished, too golden, too cold. His heart ached with the memory of the last time he was in here, with Nyra. he remembered the way she had looked up at the painting of Cedric Draymoor, lost her balance and fell over on him, and the way she laughed at his story about the giants. He could not feel her in his arms anymore, but through the walls he could hear the sounds of the people outside as her memory echoed with them, and for a moment it felt like she was there with him again.

Corwin moved slowly down the aisle, the sound of celebration outside fading behind thick stone. He stood before the towering portraits of his ancestors painted in fine robes and hollow eyes. Cedric Draymoor's image loomed largest, crown heavy on his head, and expression as cruel in paint as it had been in life.

Corwin stared at him for a long time, "**I am not you**," he whispered. He did not just say it, he *believed* it, "you were wrong in your way of ruling," he turned and looked at the rest of the portraits, "all of you were."

With a single swing, he slashed Cedric's canvas from corner to corner. Then, grabbing it with both hands, he tore it from the frame, ripping it to the top. The sound of splitting canvas echoed like thunder in the vaulted chamber. One by one, the painted monarchs fell. Wood splintering, gold leaf flaking to the floor like dried blood. Their faces, once preserved in oil paints, were slashed, erased, and obliterated.

"You ruled with fear," Corwin said through clenched teeth, driving the blade through another frame, "with arrogance and indifference." He knocked over a pedestal. Glass shattered as it crashed to the ground.

"You starved your people to feed your egos. You built a throne and forgot the ones who built *you*," another blow, another canvas torn.

"You made me believe I had to be like you to matter," he slammed the sword against the wall, the final portrait breaking clean in half. Only one portrait remained, his own.

A youth painted in oil and pride, placed there far too soon by the council eager to show the kingdom its new heir. Corwin stared at it, at the boy he once was. The version of himself who believed power had to be untouchable and who thought crowns made men noble. He let the sword fall from his hand with a dull clatter. Slowly, he reached out, running his fingers across the canvas. The paint was smooth beneath his touch, but it felt distant.

"And I believed you," he murmured, voice thick with shame. He lifted the frame from the wall, the wood creaking as he pulled it free. In his mind, he saw that day. Sunlight poured through the throne room windows, the scent of fresh parchment and oiled leather. The day he sat for the portrait. The day his father smiled at him. The first and only time he looked proud.

"You made it, Corwin," his father had said, *"you are ready to be king."* Corwin's jaw clenched.

"I am only just now ready to be king," he said through his teeth. With a sharp cry, he snapped the painting over his knee. The frame splintered with a loud crack. He hurled the pieces to the floor, where they shattered among the remains of all the others. The boy in the portrait was gone.

When Corwin stepped back outside, the light struck him differently. The air was thick with dust and sunlight. Chunks of the wall now lay scattered across the courtyard like broken teeth. The people, his people, had made incredible progress. Half the wall was already torn down, revealing glimpses of the village beyond.

Children darted between fallen stones, laughing. Elders sat on the ledge catching their breath. A woman handed a boy a hammer twice his size, and he marched off with the seriousness of a soldier. The courtyard buzzed with life and purpose.

Corwin descended the steps slowly, unnoticed at first. He walked past a toppled statue, one of some long-dead king on horseback, the head cracked off at the base. He did not look back at it. Then a man with soot-smudged cheeks turned and saw him. He paused, pickaxe resting on his shoulder.

"Your Majesty," the man said, breathless.

Corwin raised a hand, "no need for that anymore," he said, stepping down into the rubble, "just Corwin."

A quiet ripple passed through the crowd. Then someone laughed. A deep, free sound, "alright, *Corwin*," the woman grinned, tossing him a hammer. He caught it one-handed and looked down at it. He nodded once, then turned to the wall and struck a loose stone. It tumbled down, thudding into the dirt. A cheer went up behind him.

Soon, others joined him, and the rhythm picked up. The sound of stone breaking, laughter rising, and a kingdom remaking itself. Corwin looked to the horizon through the growing gap in the wall. A breeze stirred the dust. For the first time, the castle no longer felt like a prison or a throne, it felt like part of something larger. He wiped the sweat from his brow and lifted the hammer again. There was still work to be done.

Twenty Seven

What Words Could Possibly be Enough?

Corwin struck at the wall until his leg started to ache, a dull pain radiating up through the stump where flesh met wood. He let out a quiet breath, leaned on his cane, and stepped away from the commotion. Carefully, he made his way to the castle steps and lowered himself down with a tired groan.

As he adjusted his prosthetic to sit more comfortably, a familiar voice drifted beside him, "that was a very brave thing you did." Corwin turned. Agnes sat down beside him, her expression warm and knowing, the corners of her mouth pulled into a small smile.

He gave a faint smile of his own, "it was what was necessary."

"Necessary or not," she said, watching the villagers work, "most would not have had the strength to do it. You should be proud of yourself."

Corwin did not respond right away. His eyes scanned the courtyard. Dust hung in the air like mist, glowing in shafts of sunlight. The people moved through it with purpose and joy, shoulders pressed together, laughter echoing off the stone. The wall was nearly gone now, and beyond it, he could see the rooftops of the village, trees, open sky, and a future.

"I feel I owe it to them," he said quietly, "after all the pain this place has caused. After everything I let happen." He stared off into the distance as the wind brushed through his hair. The palace around them was changing, yes, in stone and structure, but something else was shifting, too. The silence that had weighed on them for so long was gone. And in its place, the breeze carried something this kingdom has rarely seen.

Hope.

He sat quietly for a while, letting it all settle in his bones. "I have been thinking," Corwin said at last, voice soft, "about going to see Nyra's aunt. To let her know what happened." Just saying the words twisted something in his chest. It all started with an apple, a laugh, a choice.

Agnes let out a dry laugh, "that is a *stupid* idea."

Corwin blinked, "pardon?"

"I mean it," she said, her smirk tinged with real affection. "Nyra's mother and her sister are the fiercest women I have ever met. If you showed up on her doorstep to tell her her niece is dead, she would skin you alive before you finished your apology."

Corwin's face fell. He looked down at his hands. "I can not just... wait for her to find out. She deserves the truth and an apology from me."

Agnes tilted her head, her smile softening into something gentler, "then write her a letter. She can not kill you if you are not there," she added with a small grin, "but your words will still reach her."

Corwin let the thought settle in his mind. He exhaled slowly, the pain and guilt still gnawing at him, but the clarity began to form, "I suppose you are right."

Agnes gave his knee a gentle pat, "I usually am."

They sat in silence for a while, watching the people swing hammers and toss rubble, working side by side as if they had done it their whole lives. Now, there was no line between castle and village. Between ruler and ruled. Corwin looked at his people, he did not feel like he was watching them from above. He was one of them now.

"Right... I am going to go write that letter now," Corwin said, pushing himself to his feet with a slight grunt.

"Just be honest," Agnes replied with a knowing smile, "Reila does not care for people who beat around the bush."

Corwin chuckled faintly, "I will. Thank you." He turned and made his way back toward the castle, cane tapping softly against the stone with each step. He did not rush. Every hallway, every column he passed carried a memory now, a shadow of her. As he ascended the staircase and turned down the long corridor to his room, his mind drifted back to the day he first brought Nyra inside these walls. She had walked beside him slowly, wide-eyed, her fingers brushing the intricate carvings in the walls, the heavy tapestries, the golden sconces lit with warm flame.

"It is like a painting," Nyra whispered.

Corwin glanced over his shoulder at her, "a cold one, I imagine."

She saw the world in ways no one else ever had. Not the castle. Not the kingdom. Not even Corwin himself. She brought a light to these halls, soft, but steady. Not to burn or blind, but to warm. In her presence, this place had finally started to feel like a home.

Now, as he walked alone through the same corridors, that warmth lingered in the quiet. Not gone, just woven into the stone he trailed his fingers across, the way she once had. Retracing her memory into the walls.

When he reached his chambers, he moved to the small table by the window. The late afternoon sun spilled across the wooden surface, illuminating dust floating gently in the stillness. Corwin sat down with a slow breath. He pulled a fresh sheet of parchment from the drawer, dipped the quill into the inkwell, and paused, his hand hovering above the page. **What words could possibly be enough?**

He thought of Nyra's laugh, the gleam in her eyes, the stubborn courage that had outshone even his own crown. He thought of her hands brushing the piano keys, her fingers curled around an apple, her smile as she stood in the garden. He exhaled, set the quill down on the parchment, and began to write.

Twenty Eight

Dear Reila

Dear Reila,

My name is Corwin Draymoor, and though you may already be familiar with who I am, I still feel it right to introduce myself properly. I am the current king of this kingdom, and I write to you as a man who has caused irreparable sorrow, and who carries that weight daily.

I have gone over these words in my mind a thousand times, never quite finding the right ones. Nothing I say will be enough, but I must speak all the same, because you deserve truth, and you deserve to hear it from me directly. This letter is not an act of formality. It is a confession, and a plea for your understanding, though I know I have no right to ask for such grace.

I am writing to you about Nyra.

Nyra came into my life in the simplest of ways. She offered me an apple, one of your apples. I remember her eyes more than anything. Curious, kind, and bright. There was something in her gaze that I had not seen in years, a sense of sincerity. That first moment led to another, and another, until I realized that my world had begun to shift around her. What began as curiosity grew into admiration, and that admiration into love, though I fear I realized it too late.

She entered this palace as a commoner and transformed it into something warmer than I ever believed it could be. In a place built on stone, politics, and cold tradition, she was the first true warmth I had ever felt. She questioned everything, challenged everything, and yet she did it with grace and a strength I had never encountered before. She was not afraid of me, or my title. She saw past all of it, and that was a gift I never deserved. But I failed her.

I did not protect her when she needed me most. I stood in rooms where her name was twisted into poison, where her presence was called a threat, and though I fought for her, I did not fight hard enough. I let fear take root where trust should have bloomed. I let politics and power distract me from what truly mattered. And when it mattered most, I was not fast enough, nor strong enough.

Nyra was taken from this world in an execution of fire and ash. The very people who claimed loyalty to me turned their backs on everything I tried to build. They silenced her voice with cruelty and ignorance. She died because she dared to be different. Because she dared to be loved by someone who was supposed to be above her. Because I could not keep her safe.

Her final moments are etched into me, and I live them every night in my dreams I cannot escape. I remember the sound of her voice, and the feel of her hand slipping away from mine. I remember the weight of her ashes on my robes. I kept them.

Reila, I am sorry. More than words can hold. More than parchment can contain. I imagine you raised her with strength, because she was strong in every fiber of her being. I imagine you taught her to be kind, because she had a gentleness that could soothe storms. I imagine you loved her fiercely. I hope you did. Because she deserved it. She deserved everything.

I do not write this letter to beg forgiveness, I know that may never come. I only wish for you to know that she mattered. Not because she was loved by a king, but because she was Nyra. Brilliant, brave, and good. Her death has broken me in ways I cannot repair. And yet, through that breaking, something new has begun to take shape.

In her name, I have torn down the very walls that separated the people of this kingdom. I have stripped away the titles and traditions that buried so many voices. I have handed over the crown in spirit and placed it in the hands of the people. This kingdom will not be ruled as it was before. It will be guided. Built from the ground up. With compassion, equity, and truth. She taught me that.

You may never wish to speak to me. You may hate me, and if you do, I will carry that hate with grace, because it is no less than I deserve. But if you should ever find your way to my gates know that you will always be welcome here. Not as a visitor or a stranger, but as an honor.

I will never stop grieving for her. But I will honor her, every day, by creating the world she deserved to live in.

With deepest sorrow,
Corwin Draymoor

Corwin rolled up the parchment with care, the edges trembling slightly in his hands. He reached for the wax seal, melting it over a small flame until it pooled over the seam. Then, with steady fingers, he pressed the Draymoor crest into the wax.

He set the scroll down gently and sat in silence for a moment, his chest rising and falling with quiet, uneven breaths. Tears clung to his lashes, hot against his cheeks. He gathered the letter and stepped out into the hall, his cane tapping lightly as he made his way down the corridor.

He found a courier at the outer gate, "to a woman named Reila. She lives on the northern outskirts of the Montague Kingdom. You are to place this into her hands only."

The boy took the letter with both hands and nodded, "right away."

Corwin smiled faintly, "thank you." He watched the courier ride off into the horizon, the letter secure against his chest.

Twenty Nine

She is Still Here

The days drifted by. Some passed in the blink of an eye, others stretched endlessly, like years packed into hours. Time moved differently now, measured not in court meetings or commands, but in bricks laid, hands held, and lives changed.

Corwin had barely rested. He spent his days moving through the villages, sleeves rolled up, sweat on his brow, helping wherever he could, hauling stones, guiding repairs, resolving disputes, sharing meals. The sun beat down mercilessly. The height of summer had turned the earth hot and dry, but the people worked harder than ever. Side by side, shoulder to shoulder.

Under his guidance, resources were distributed evenly. Food, water, clothes, tools, everything flowed freely, with careful oversight and strategic reserves in place for emergencies. Years spent locked away in the castle's vast libraries, pouring over books no one thought he would use, had finally paid off. Numbers, systems, political plans. He turned knowledge into compassion, and theory into action.

Now, nearly two months later, the kingdom was transformed. There were no walls anymore, no gates, no guards standing between the castle and the village, because there was no longer a need. Every family had a sturdy roof above their head. Clothes that fit. Food that filled their bellies. Water that ran clear and cool. The kingdom was filled with safety, community, dignity, and peace.

Corwin stood one evening at the edge of the old courtyard, now transformed into a lively gathering space. Lanterns flickered in the twilight, children chased each other through open walkways, and the scent of baked bread and spiced stew filled the air. He looked out over all of it, heart full. This was the kingdom he had always dreamed of. A kingdom *they* had dreamed of. And it stood here now, because of one girl.

"Corwin!" a voice called out, and a guard ran up to him, though now he was no longer covered in clanking armor or wielding a weapon. He wore a simple uniform, hand-stitched and proudly worn, designed by a young woman from the village.

"Yes?" Corwin turned to face him.

"There is someone in the village looking for you," the guard said between breaths, placing a hand on Corwin's shoulder to steady himself, "a woman from another kingdom, said you would know who she is." Corwin's heart dropped. He knew exactly who it was.

"Thank you, Herren," he said quickly, tapping the man's shoulder before turning on his heel and making his way down the path into the heart of the village. He moved quickly, weaving through the growing evening crowd, his pulse loud in his ears. When he reached the town square, he spotted her.

She was speaking with Agnes, who wore a gentle smile. The woman beside her had long dark hair and the same icy, penetrating eyes Nyra once had, but her cheeks were fuller, her skin warmer with color. She moved like someone with weight in her step, someone who had fought and survived.

Agnes was the first to spot him. She touched the woman's arm and nodded in his direction. Reila turned and in an instant, she knew. So did he. Corwin felt something in his chest both rise and crack. She reminded him so much of Nyra it hurt.

She stepped toward him with deliberate, confident strides. Corwin took a slow breath, ready to greet her with the respect she was due. But before he could utter a word, her palm cracked hard across his face. The sharp sting spread across his cheek. His hand slowly came up to the red mark.

"That is for your arrogant ass," Reila snapped, "for taking my niece into your castle like she was some shiny new toy you got to pick out." Corwin did not argue. He bowed his head, eyes to the ground. He deserved it, every bit of her rage. But Reila's fire faded as quickly as it had ignited. Her face crumpled, and in the next breath, she threw her arms around his neck and pulled him into a tight embrace. Corwin froze for half a second, then wrapped his arms around her carefully like she was something sacred. Agnes chuckled quietly behind them.

Reila pulled back just enough to look at him, eyes glassy but strong, "but you are also just a man. One who was raised in the shadow of a broken system, who made mistakes, and did not know how to fix them. But I see you now, Corwin. I see the world you are trying to build. This place, this kingdom, it already looks and *feels* so different than it used to."

Her voice softened, cracking just slightly, "that makes you a good man, and damn it, a great king." Corwin's throat tightened.

"My heart is at peace knowing Nyra spent her final day with you. Thank you... for loving my girl. Even if it did not end well. All she ever wanted was someone to *listen*. Someone to see her." She glanced around the village square, at the people sharing food, children playing without fear, music drifting from open windows.

"If she could see this," Reila whispered, "her heart would be soaring." Tears welled in her eyes, but she did not let them fall.

Corwin's voice came low, thick with emotion, "she built this with me, Reila. Every stone. Every bit of it. **She is still here.**"

Reila nodded, her hand brushing his arm, "I know."

Agnes stepped closer, joining them with a familiar twinkle in her eye, "Reila has brought you a gift."

Reila's face lit up, her earlier emotion replaced by sudden delight, "oh! I almost forgot!"

She hurried off toward the horse-drawn carriage that had brought her to the village, her skirt gathering dust as she moved. Corwin watched, curious. She reached the back of the cart and yanked aside a large linen sheet, revealing a massive, colorful mound of apples.

Corwin's jaw dropped. He stepped forward, eyes wide. Reds, golds, and soft greens gleamed in the evening light, still speckled with orchard dust and warm from the sun. The smell hit him next, sweet, crisp, familiar. He remembered those apples perfectly. The way Nyra had casually handed him one like it was nothing, only for it to be the most delicious fruit he had ever tasted.

"For me?" he asked, voice almost boyish with awe.

"For *everyone*," Reila said with a proud smile, "use them however you like. Nyra always loved sharing her apples. Said she wanted the people of this kingdom to know how good they were... but I think she just liked showing off." She laughed, wiping her eyes with the back of her hand.

Corwin chuckled, his smile widening, "in her defense... they *are* show-off worthy." They both laughed then, a real, light-hearted laughter. The kind that rises out of grief not because it forgets, but because it remembers with joy. He looked at the apples again, as the wind passed gently through the square. A gift, symbol, and memory made edible. Suddenly, he had an idea.

"Why don't we throw a celebration?" Corwin said suddenly, his eyes lighting up, "for the rebirth of the kingdom, and to honor Nyra."

Agnes's smile widened with recognition, "just like the parties your mother used to host."

Corwin's expression softened, "yes... just like her parties." Agnes placed a hand gently over the locket around her neck, her fingers curling around it with reverence. Her eyes shimmered with memory.

"That sounds perfect," Reila said, looping an arm around Agnes's shoulder with a warm grin.

"You seem to be especially fond of my mother's parties," Corwin said, unable to hide his amusement as he watched Agnes beam uncontrollably.

"One of your mother's parties," she said with a fond sigh, "is where I met my husband."

Corwin chuckled, "then it is settled. There shall be a celebration at the end of the week."

"I will help in the kitchens," Reila chimed in, "I have a few good party dishes in mind, and a few better ones if I have wine while cooking."

"That explains a lot," Agnes teased with a playful nudge, "I can perform. Oh, how I have missed playing the piano for an audience."

Corwin looked at the two women, the strength, the memory, the laughter between them, and felt a fullness in his chest that words could not hold.

"Yes," he said quietly, smiling, "let us celebrate for everything we have lost and everything we have begun."

Thirty

Thank You For Everything

The night of the celebration arrived, warm and golden, with the sky painted in soft hues of pink and lavender. The sun dipped low over the horizon as the final rays of light kissed the rooftops of a kingdom reborn. Lanterns glowed from every corner of the courtyard, strung between castle towers and village houses. Long tables lined the square, draped in fresh table cloths and covered with food.

The air was rich with the scent of roasting meats, sweet breads, and spiced apple dishes that filled the entire kingdom with the aroma of harvest. Reila had kept her word. Every variety of apple was used: baked into pies, stewed with cinnamon, candied, sliced fresh and drizzled with honey, even pressed into sparkling cider that flowed like wine.

Children danced barefoot beneath the lantern light, their laughter echoing into the night. Elders clapped along to the music, while neighbors who had once barely spoken now shared plates and stories like lifelong friends. There were no divisions, no barriers, only joy.

At the heart of the ballroom sat the grand piano, the same one that had been played by both Corwin's mother and Nyra. Now Agnes sat upon the bench, her fingers positioned with grace and memory. When she began to play, silence gently swept over the crowd. The melody was tender, familiar, the same song Nyra had once played for Corwin late into the night.

Corwin stood off to the side, watching the people with soft eyes. His cane rested beside him, but he did not lean on it. He stood tall, whole in a way that had nothing to do with limbs or crowns. As the song carried through the ballroom, he stepped forward. He met Agnes's gaze, and she gave a small nod before continuing to play. Then, Corwin did something he had never done before.

"Not yet, but if you ever do… sing for me."

His voice was quiet at first, uncertain, but it found its rhythm, growing stronger with each note. He sang of a girl with wild eyes and a laugh that could warm the coldest heart. Of a kingdom that had forgotten how to feel. Of love that burned, and loss that shaped the world. And of a hope that grew like a seed in broken earth.

Singing came surprisingly easy to him. He guessed it must have been from all those years of hearing his mother sing. The words fell from his mouth like a bird soaring high in the sky, a falcon above the stars. He let the sound of the music fill his ears and heal his heart.

For a moment he could see his mother dancing around the room in one of her extravagant gowns. Smiling bright and lively with her contagious aura. For a moment he could see Nyra on the bench next to Agnes, her fingers gliding across the keyboard like silk on glass. Her talents filled the room with a beauty that healed the heart of everyone around. For a moment Agnes could see her husband for the first time smiling with a drink in his hand. He lived not for a purpose or a destiny but to have fun and enjoy the present. For a moment Reila could just sit back and relax watching everyone compliment her apples she worked all year to grow. For a moment Elowyn could see her hard work being paid off as people sunk their teeth into her foods she poured her whole heart and soul into. Her husband standing tall over her as he leaned down to kiss the top of her head. For a moment Seren forgot about the day her parents died and the former king casted her out of the castle. She smiled, thankful for the second chance she was given.

For a moment everything was perfect. Corwin knew he could never change the world but he could change this kingdom, he has. He has watched his home transform in front of his own eyes into something magical. The throne expanded into a bench where everyone was allowed to sit. It was no longer about one man but instead one nation. This is the world they all deserved. This is the kingdom Nyra deserved.

Later into the night, as the music gave way to soft laughter and the tables emptied of their feast, Corwin stepped away. He wandered into the garden, past the stone where his mother and Nyra now rested, and knelt in the quiet. He carried a wide smile on his face and a slight rosiness in his cheeks from the apple bourbon Reila had made.

"Thank you for everything," he whispered, "for showing me how to love and how to lead. This kingdom needed you. I needed you. You changed everything, Nyra. You broke through walls I did not even know I had. You taught me that love is not weakness, but strength. That power is not in titles, but in compassion. I used to think I had to be like my father to rule. But you... you showed me another way. A better way." He picked one perfect apple from the basket Reila had left behind, sat cross-legged beneath the moonlight, and took a bite, sweet, bright, and alive. He did not speak, but just sat with his mother and Nyra. The stars twinkled high in the sky with the moon casting mystical silvery beams across the garden. It made him feel small. It reminded him that the world is so much bigger than the castle walls he was raised in. That there are people of all different families and traditions getting by day after day. Everyone has their own path in life but in the end no one is really that different from each other. We all just want to be loved, and to have someone listen to us.

When he finished, he tossed the core into the soft soil. Over time, the earth slowly closed over it. Though no one else saw it, Corwin smiled. Because he knew one day, there would be a tree, and under it, someone would fall in love again.

"Thank you for everything."

Forbidden Snow

A thank you to my aunt who gave me the dress used for the front cover. A sweet woman who is like a second mother to me, much like Agnes was to Nyra and Corwin.

And thank you to my boyfriend who gave me a lot of inspiration for Corwin's "new" kingdom. I love you too.

www.ingramcontent.com/pod-product-compliance
Lightning Source LLC
LaVergne TN
LVHW012022060526
838201LV00061B/4419